Rusty Wilson's Mysterious Bigfoot Campfire Stories

Forward

by Rusty Wilson

Greetings, fellow adventurers, to this set of sixteen all new Bigfoot campfire stories, stories guaranteed to either make you smile or scare the socks off you.

I've put this collection together for those of you who enjoy the more mysterious side of Bigfootery. If you've read my other books, you'll know that you're in for a treat if you enjoy Bigfoot, mystery, and adventure, and most people who love one also love the others.

These stories were collected around many campfires, where my flyfishing clients regaled and scared me to death with their Bigfoot encounters. It always amazes me how many people have had Bigfoot encounters. There are many mysteries on this planet, and I think they make life interesting.

Of course, nothing compares to the mysterious world of Bigfoot, a world we humans rarely get a glimpse into—but when we do, it often results in a huge paradigm shift. We begin to realize there are many things we don't yet know, and so many really good mysteries.

So, pull up a chair or log, kick back with some hot chocolate, and be prepared to hear some tales that will make your hair stand on end—or make you wonder if you might like to meet the Big Guy himself.

The Bigfoot Campground Host

I rarely stay in campgrounds, as I prefer the peace and quiet of boondocking, staying out in the wilds. But I must say I've always thought campgrounds would be safer than going it on your own, but now I'm not so sure.

I met Lou on a guided trip on the Gallatin in Montana, and I was really intrigued by his idea of Bigfoot being a campground host, though I sure wouldn't want to hang out in that particular campground. —Rusty

I was about 23 and had a seasonal job working on a trail crew for the Forest Service in northern California. It was hard work, and there were about a dozen of us, all in good shape and gung-ho and happy to spend our summer camping out and getting paid for it, though the pay wasn't that great. But the stories that came out of that one summer, man, they're something else.

One of the guys fell off a small bridge we were building across a stream, then another got conked on the head by deadfall when we were thinning out some trees, then another got lost—well, you get the picture. Nobody was seriously injured or anything, but it was probably the most memorable three months of my life, and that's saying something, since I'm now a smoke jumper.

But the most amazing story of that entire summer was the one where we had a Bigfoot for a campground host. It's kind of funny in retrospect, but at the time, man, it was awful.

Now, maybe you're not aware of the position of campground host, so let me describe it a bit, at least how it works in the Forest Service. It's a volunteer position, and the person or couple doing it gets a free camp spot for the summer in what are usually some of the country's best campgrounds—I mean, really beautiful places. Plus, they sometimes get a bit of a stipend to help with their expenses, and they have rangers keeping an eye out for them, which provides a little security.

In exchange, they supervise the campground and make sure everyone follows the rules—things like quiet hour and picking up the trash and stuff like that. It's a pretty nice gig if you can get it and you have the right disposition to deal with people and all their foibles—and I do mean foibles. Actually, that's the nice word for it, as some would call it inconsideration and downright cantankerousness. Only the bigger campgrounds—the more popular ones—usually have campground hosts.

We had spent part of the summer camping up in a meadow, building this footbridge for hikers, as the previous spring it had washed out, shutting down a very popular trail. So at first we weren't even in a campground. It was nice and quiet.

But once we got that done, we moved down into lower country and stayed in a real campground, one with a campground host, such that he was. And this guy, the campground host, he was pretty lazy. I don't think he came back the following season—in fact, I know he didn't. I guess he didn't like the idea of a Bigfoot showing him how to do his job.

OK, so here we were, a dozen young guys all working hard by day and drinking a few beers after dinner around a campfire, then hitting the hay, exhausted. We were too tired to party, and we had no tolerance for anyone who did. We wanted to sleep at night because we had to get up early and do the same thing all over again the next day, working our tail ends off.

We were camped on the far side of the campground, in an area for tenters, and our group pretty much took up that whole area. The rest of the campground was open to tents or RVs, but it seemed to be full of mostly big RVs.

That was the summer I learned to hate generators, because these guys would be there in the middle of one of the most beautiful places on earth and be sitting inside watching TV, running their generators with no regard for what the noise and pollution was doing to the rest of us.

The campground had rules for when you could run these generator beasts, but the host was camped clear over on the opposite side from the RVs and it seemed he couldn't hear them, or else he just didn't care. Every single night, someone would have to go get him to shut down the generators so we could sleep, sometimes hours after quiet time.

He always acted like whoever complained was the problem. It got really old, and this was probably the start of all the tension that began to build up and later resulted in a big explosion, though it wasn't the kind you make with dynamite.

We had been pretty easy-going and tolerant—other than the generators—but one weekend a big party came in with several campers and RVs of all sizes and shapes. They had reserved the group site, which really wasn't that close to the tent sites where we were, so all of what happened shouldn't have been much of a problem, though it was, as you'll see.

This party appeared to be a bunch of friends from Reno, Nevada, which one of our guys found out by talking to them. There were a half-dozen couples, and you could tell this was a big deal for them. They obviously intended to make the most of it and have maximum fun.

They seemed to be fairly well-heeled and had really nice rigs—things like a newer Gulfstream trailer and a really nice Bigfoot camper (which I found to be really ironic, given what happened), along with a couple of those Mercedes Sprinter vans. They also had tons of gear, including barbecues, big screen tents for the mosquitos, and plenty of generators.

I have no idea how much money all those rigs and stuff represented, but I'd bet my next paycheck that it was more than all our salaries put together for many years. It sure made our little tents seem inconsequential, but when all was said and done, we were actually the ones with the best defense, which was the defense of laying low, as you'll soon see.

They came rolling in after we'd finished work for the day. We were eating a big spaghetti dinner and having a few Bud Lites, which was pretty much our standard. It wasn't dark, and we all just sat there watching across the campground as these guys came in and set up their rigs and their tents and chairs and all their special stuff, the whole place looking like an Israeli army encampment when they were done.

They then started grilling something that smelled really good, and one of our guys said it was bratwurst. Well, they must've also had some really good alcohol, too, because it wasn't long before they were sitting around a big fire and talking really loud, which soon turned into laughing and hooting and hollering, while their kids—and there were a bunch of them—ran around screaming like banshees. They had pretty much taken over the campground, and it hadn't taken them long to do it.

We didn't want to spoil their fun, but they were getting louder and louder as we got sleepier and sleepier. We wanted to go to bed, and the official quiet hour started at 10 p.m. It was now 10:30 and nobody had even bothered to say a word to them. The campground host's trailer was dead—no lights, as usual. Someone would have to go wake him up if we wanted to get any sleep. I think he must've slept with earplugs.

I got the vote since it was my turn, so I trudged over to his little trailer and pounded on the door. He finally got up, and after I told him the problem, he begrudgingly said he'd go talk to them. He was a small guy with a big pot belly, and he was never nice to anyone—he was just an old curmudgeon. Not much of a host.

I went back to the campfire, where we all sat and waited. A few of the guys were already in their tents, trying to sleep as the party got louder and louder.

Did I mention the dogs? They all had dogs, and I'm a dog lover, but these dogs were just like their owners. As things got louder and louder, the dogs barked more and more. I guess they were excited by it all.

They were running around all over the place, and a pair of black labs came over to visit our camp, peeing on everything we had. We soon encouraged them to go home, but they had to visit all the other campers on their way back.

This made me worry, as dogs aren't usually savvy about the dangers in the wilds, and we'd heard a pack of coyotes howling several times on previous nights. Before I worry anyone, I'll say the dogs were all fine and came out of all this a bit wiser, but OK.

See, I'm the kind of guy that if the animals get hurt, I don't want to hear the story, so there you go. No animals were harmed in the making of this story. Ha. But a few human egos definitely were.

OK, on with the story. We sat and waited, but the campground host had obviously gone back to bed. At least that's what it seemed like, as the light in his trailer went out and he never came out of the door and the party didn't subside one bit. Some campground host. He was a total shirker.

We could see that other campers were getting upset, too, and finally some of them went and talked to the bunch, who then started quieting down. By then, it was really late.

Boy, were we all hot under the collar. Some of us lay there in our sleeping bags and devised ways to get even with them at dawn, when we'd be getting up. Things like "accidentally" setting off our car alarms, that kind of thing.

But of course when dawn came, we didn't have the heart to do anything, as we knew we'd also wake up everyone else. So, we just dragged ourselves out of bed and drank lots of coffee and headed wearily up the trail, where we were building water bars to help keep the trail from eroding out. Water bars are kind of like little dams in the trail that channel the water off it.

We worked hard that day, and our sleep deprivation caught up with us with a vengeance. Combined with the heat, it all made for a pretty tired bunch when we dragged ourselves back into camp that evening, exhausted.

We had foil dinners and sat around the fire eating them. Foil dinners are when you wrap your food—stuff like hamburger and potatoes—in foil and cook it over hot coals. We always ate a lot of foil dinners, as they were good and also easy to clean up—just throw everything away when you were done. Just fling it, which is just my style.

Well, the neighbors across the way were once again cooking something pretty tasty smelling. It smelled like barbecued ribs, and they were putting out a lot of smoke with their barbecues.

Everything over there was quiet, and we hoped the noise yesterday was just from their first day of excitement at being out. Maybe they'd worn themselves out during the day and would go to bed early.

Well, no such luck. After they all finished dinner, the kids started up screaming at each other again, the adults began hooting and hollering, and the dogs began making their rounds. We all groaned, but it got worse. The kids now started driving around the campground on ATVs, no helmets or anything, and a couple of them couldn't have been more than five or six years old.

Round and round and round they went, making more noise than even the night before. Finally, when they came around our loop for the umpteenth time, one of our guys went out and stopped them, telling them that if they came by there again, he was going to take their ATVs away. He was really mad.

OK, that was a big mistake, because pretty soon, here came a couple of the dads. Oh boy. They started yelling at us and swearing and threatening to call the rangers on us. I found that really ironic as hell, given that it was totally illegal for anyone under eight to be riding an ATV, especially without a helmet.

It looked like it was going to come to a fistfight, so I went over to the campground host's trailer. After I pounded on the door for a while, he finally came out and reluctantly went over and talked everyone into settling down, telling the noisemakers that the kids couldn't be riding the ATVs around the campground like that.

It was the first time he'd said anything to them, and he acted like he was really put out for having to do his job. He even gave me a dirty look. I knew then for sure he hadn't even bothered to talk to them last night.

Man, I was starting to get really mad. I was about ready to go find a ranger, though I wasn't sure where to start looking. I knew the campground host had a radio, but I also knew he wouldn't let me use it.

OK, things settled down for a bit, and we'd all just climbed into our tents when they started up again. The kids were screaming, and the adults were laughing and shouting. I looked at my watch. It was 10:30, a half-hour past quiet time.

I finally drifted off to sleep in spite of the noise, as I was exhausted, but about an hour later the dogs were over sniffing around my tent and woke me up.

I sat up and thought about everything. This is a problem, I thought, and all problems have solutions. How could I solve this one? I pondered it and finally came up with an idea.

I crawled out of my tent and went and got James, the guy who'd threatened to take away the ATVs. I knew he was mad enough to help me out.

He thought it was a good idea, so we set off to implement it. We snuck out through the thick trees a good couple of hundred feet from camp, then found some big sticks and started doing this woodknocking thing that Bigfoot supposedly do. Even though we'd heard about this, none of us believed in Bigfoot one bit, as we'd all been in the forests a lot and never seen or heard anything.

OK, that turned out to be a bust, because they were making so much noise they didn't even hear us. We were hoping they'd get scared and go to bed, but no such luck. We stood there for a while, then started making these whooping noises and screams and whatever we could come up with that sounded scary. In fact, we were kind of scaring ourselves.

They acted like they didn't hear that, either, so we finally gave up and went back to our tents. Everyone in our group had gone to bed, but a few other people around the campground were still up, and we could hear them talking. They sounded like they'd heard the so-called Bigfoot and were wondering what was going on.

We sat there and talked for a while, trying to come up with some other means to shut the noise down, but it seemed hopeless. It was now after eleven and the party was just getting started. The campground host's lights were out—in more ways than one, I figured.

Oh man, this guy, James—the one who had helped me make the noises—he was getting madder and madder by the minute. I thought he was going to pop a cork. He started over to the other camp, but I stopped him. I knew it would probably turn into another big confrontation.

We sat there, steaming mad, as the noise continued on. By now, some of the other campers had gone over and talked to the noisy bunch, but with no results. A couple of other guys from my bunch were up and pacing around, trying to figure out what to do.

Well, before long, these guys got together and concocted a plan. They would wait until the noisy party all went to bed, then go over to their camp and "borrow" their barbecues, take them into the woods, and hide them. Maybe the group would get the picture the next morning when they got up and found they couldn't cook breakfast.

I wasn't too sure this was a good idea and said so. I told them it might be a recipe for getting shot, but the guys didn't care, they were just wanting revenge at that point. I decided to sit that one out.

Well, it was about midnight when the noise kind of settled down, and I was in my tent, listening and wondering if the guys were still going to execute their plan. I hoped they'd all gone to sleep, but I soon heard whispering and the sound of footsteps, so I knew they were still on it.

They hadn't been gone more than a few minutes when I heard someone screaming, then I heard a crashing through the bushes near our tents and could see a blue light nearby, kind of shaking and moving like someone carrying a headlamp and running through the forest.

I jumped up, pulled on my pants and boots, grabbed my headlamp, and was soon out of my tent. There stood our campground host in his BVDs, shaking like a leaf and looking like he was about ready to cry, muttering something about a bear hitting the side of his trailer and trying to break in, and how he managed to run away when it headed over to the RV sites. Man, this guy was scared to death. I was glad I wasn't depending on him for backup in a tight situation.

I wanted to laugh at the justice of him being awakened in the middle of the night, but I also kind of felt sorry for him because he was so scared. I was wondering where the bear had gone and hoped nobody was in danger.

I asked if anyone had seen James and the other guys who were going to play the prank—if you could call it that—on the noisy campers, but nobody had seen them, and they were apparently still gone.

OK, I knew then that they were the so-called "bear" and had scared the campground host, probably in retribution for his attitude and lack of responsibility. Whatever they'd done, it had worked. I was now laughing to myself.

I stood there talking to the host for a while, telling him it was just a prank and that the guys were pretty mad at him for not doing his job. He was real quiet, then finally agreed he needed to do better and said he would, so I walked him back over to his trailer. He went inside and turned on all the lights. I figured he was still a bit scared, even though he now knew it was a prank.

When I got back to the tents, James and the guys were there laughing and cracking up at the prank they'd just pulled. It seems they'd managed to sneak into the RV sites where the noisy campers were and haul their barbecues over into the trees a ways off.

I was pretty mad at the noisy campers just like everyone else was, but I kind of considered this prank a little over the top, as it seemed to me like theft. How would they find their barbecues? Was James going to eventually tell them where they were hidden when all was said and done? Somehow I suspected he wasn't, though it did seem like it served them right.

I shrugged my shoulders and went to bed, sleeping like a log.

The next day was uneventful, and we were long gone by the time the noisy campers got up and discovered their barbecues were gone, so none of us had the pleasure of seeing their reaction.

But I did get to see the reaction of James and his cohorts when the ranger came by, looking for the thieves. It seems the campers had reported the missing stuff. I was glad I hadn't been involved.

James denied responsibility, which I thought was another bad decision on his part, though I could see where he was coming from. After the ranger left, James told me they were going to put everything back that night after everyone went to sleep. I guess seeing the ranger made him a bit uncomfortable.

Seems like the prank had kind of backfired, and the noisy bunch was still there, even though everyone had hoped they would leave.

It was a quiet evening, and we sat around the campfire, eating more foil dinners, when talk drifted to the night before. Everyone in our bunch knew what James and his buddies had done, but nobody was inclined to feel any sorrow over it on behalf of the victims, including me. It had apparently had the desired outcome, for even though the noisemakers were still there, they were being relatively quiet.

But I'll never forget the chill I felt when someone mentioned how scared the campground host had been when they hit his trailer. James looked surprised and said they hadn't been anywhere near the trailer.

We all sat there, then tried to figure out what it could've been. I had decided it had to have been a bear, but someone pointed out that bears wouldn't do that kind of thing as they didn't use their paws like that.

I thought of how I'd walked all alone back through the forest the previous night after I'd helped the host home, and I felt kind of spooked. That bear or whatever it was could've been right there, looking at me, within claw's reach, and I'd been totally unaware.

I knew that making assumptions could easily lead to disaster out here where humans weren't necessarily the apex predator—and what if it hadn't been a bear? I felt an even bigger chill when I thought of James and me out there in the dark, woodknocking and making weird noises.

OK, I had trouble sleeping again that night, but it wasn't because of noise. I was rarely worried about being in the forest, as I'd never before thought about anything trying to harm me. We'd had a few run-ins with black bears, but they always took off the other direction. Being with a large group was a sort of protection in itself, and bears never messed with groups of people, as bears were too smart.

But what if there were something else out there? Something that could slap the side of a trailer? Yikes. The more I lay there, the more freaked I got. I finally got up, got dressed, and went out and sat in my camp chair there by the fire ring. I felt less scared out there where I could see around me, unlike in my tent.

And as I sat there, I heard something weird. It sounded like metal being twisted and smashed against rocks, and it came from over by where James had said they'd hid the barbecues.

I quietly went to James' tent and woke him up, telling him to come outside. Once he was awake to where he could process what was going on, he looked pretty freaked.

"It's that bear thingy again," I said.

"Yeah, it's probably attracted by all the grease and stuff from their cooking," he answered.

"I thought maybe it was you guys over there taking the stuff back like you said you were going to," I replied.

"We set our alarms to go off at two, then we were going over there to do just that. But now, I dunno."

We sat there, listening, when all of a sudden a rock came pelting in, almost hitting James.

He jumped up, shouting, "Hey, knock it off!"

Another rock came in, almost hitting me, then we heard a deep growl that startled me right up out of my chair. It was very deep-chested, and that chest had to be huge to make a sound that guttural and loud.

It growled for a good five or six seconds, then we could hear what sounded like something pacing back and forth in the trees, breaking twigs and limbs as it went.

The pacing was very deliberate and it sounded bipedal. Whatever was making it had to be huge, as it made the ground shake a bit—it had to be pretty close to us.

James and I just stood there in shock. We had nowhere to run and hide, so we just stood there. My instinct was to wake everyone up, but I decided against it, and soon whatever it was stomped away into the forest and all was still.

Of course there would be no more sleep for us that night. We gathered some wood from nearby and started a big fire and both sat there as close to it as we could. By dawn, we were both totally fried, happy to see the sun coming up over the horizon. It had been a long night, and James hadn't returned the barbecues, but at that point, he didn't care.

I don't know how I made it through the day. I did manage to take a nap at lunch, which helped. James looked pretty haggard himself, and I figured we would both sleep well that night, regardless of how much noise came from the bunch across the way. Of course, I didn't figure on another visit from our "bear," which I should have.

Sure enough, that night the noisy party was back at it, and it appeared they'd found their barbecues. I guess they weren't too badly damaged, as they were cooking up a storm of something that smelled like hamburgers with barbecue sauce. It appeared that most of the other campers had left.

I didn't even care. I ate some dinner and crawled into my sleeping bag, which I'd taken from my tent and put over by the fire ring. James had told the guys earlier what we'd heard, and a number of them looked kind of spooked. I figured I might have some company there by the fire when everyone decided to go to bed, as they all said they felt uncomfortable sleeping in their tents.

They built a good fire and sat around talking, but I was soon fast asleep. I recall hearing a lot of noise coming from across the campground, where it sounded like they were now playing loud music, some kind of Mexican mariachi thing, even though they weren't Mexicans. I didn't care and just crashed out without a thought.

I don't know what woke me, nor did I know what time it was, but some instinct told me to be very still. And as I lay there, scrunched down in my bag, I could see other bodies sleeping around the fire, which had burned down into nothing but coals that now glowed in the dark.

I remember thinking the fire looked like a tiny city all on fire, the coals all glowing like little buildings. It seemed like a strange thought, but I realized later it was my mind trying to distract me from what was going on.

As I lay as still as could be, I could hear noise coming from across the campground and knew the party was still going strong. People were yelling, and it sounded like they were drunk. Every once in a while a dog would join in, barking and yipping. I couldn't believe how totally out of control they were and how oblivious the campground host was to it all.

Just then, I heard someone whisper.

"Don't move, Lou. There's a Bigfoot standing right over there."

It was James, whose sleeping bag was near mine. He must've been afraid of going to his tent like I had been.

I looked over into the trees beyond the fire ring and saw nothing, but then I heard it—something big was now walking through the nearby woods, making no attempt to be stealthy, breaking twigs and branches and crushing dry leaves as it went by.

I'm no Bigfoot enthusiast and really never believed in them before this, but there's something different about seeing one for yourself. As anyone who's ever seen them will tell you, everything changes the moment you're faced with one. I was able to write everything off to a possible bear before this, but now I knew differently.

We could now hear it grunting and growling, that same deep throaty growl that had scared us both the previous night, but now it seemed oblivious to us and was soon on past.

Wherever it was going, it sounded mad—really mad. It even broke some large branches as it stomped through the timber. It sounded like it was getting ready to raise hell.

As it made its way on past us, I got a glimpse of it silhouetted against the night sky. All I could make out was a huge shadowy figure, but it had a rounded head with a crest on it, and I could see very long hairy arms hanging down to its knees. I couldn't see any more than that because it was too dark and also because the forest blocked the rest of it. It was more than I wanted to see, believe me.

Well, raise hell it did. It wasn't but a few moments later when the noisy camper crowd began screaming, and I knew the Bigfoot had to have entered their camp. It then began screaming too, a sound that made all human screams seem puny in comparison.

All was immediately silent, and I suspected everyone had made a run for their trailers. But soon, the creature was grunting and making a lot of noise, and I could hear what sounded like barbecues being flung through the air and smashing against trailers.

This went on for a few minutes, then we could hear it grunting and carrying on as it headed for the campground host's trailer. As it went by, we heard it once again smack the side of the trailer with such force that I wondered if it hadn't smashed a big hole in it.

The Bigfoot made its way back into the forest, and, as if to punctuate how angry it was, it then came back with a big tree that it threw into the middle of the campground. I wondered if that wasn't its way of telling everyone that what they'd seen was indeed real and not a figment of their drunken imaginations. And now the whole campground was deathly silent, as if in the eye of a hurricane.

I lay there for a while, almost shaking. I wanted desperately to stay awake, but I just couldn't. I was too exhausted from all the previous nights of sleep deprivation, and I somehow knew the creature wouldn't be back—at least not that night. I slept like a baby, which I never would've predicted, given the circumstances.

When I got up the next morning, the campground was empty, except for our group. Nary a soul was there, including the campground host. Everyone had fled except us. Nobody had heard them leave, as we'd all been too tired.

We were still a bit shocked from the previous night's happenings, but I will say we were all kind of reveling in the peace and quiet.

It stayed that way the entire rest of the time we were there, and even the guys in my group were abnormally quiet.

I'm pretty sure nobody wanted another visit from our new campground host.

Uncle Wally's Neighbors

I was guiding a flyfishing trip on the Green River near Flaming Gorge Dam in northeast Utah, at a place called Little Hole, when I heard this story from a gal called Sassy. It was quite the tale, and it made me feel really sorry for these creatures when they get old—they don't have a home they can go to when they get all stoved up. Too bad they don't all have someone like Sassy to help them out. —Rusty

My name is Sassy—well, it's not my real name, but rather, my nickname. I've been called that since I was a kid, and I guess it kind of fits, as I never do things like most normal people would, but I have to do them with an attitude.

That attitude has helped me in many ways, but it has also sometimes been a hindrance. I think this story is one case where it kind of helped me get through a very strange and unsettling period of my life, one I kind of hate to think about. But maybe retelling it will help me come to grips with it better.

My mom always told me I was stubborn, and I guess that's where the nickname came from. Seems I was good at arguing with her and anybody else who tried to tell me what to do. My nickname had originally been Sissy, but it evolved into Sassy.

For example, when I was 16 and old enough to drive, I decided I wanted a motorcycle instead of a car. All the other girls were getting cars, but I wanted a bike. Both my mom and dad told me motorcycles were too dangerous and there was no way I was getting one. I was really upset, because I knew if I'd been a boy, I would've had one.

So, I got a job on the weekends at the local grocery store and finally bought myself an old motorcycle that barely ran. My Uncle Wally let me secretly keep it in his garage, and he also helped me fix it up.

We both knew we'd be in trouble if my parents found out, but he was a good guy and always encouraged me to follow my heart, and he knew about not being able to do what you want, as he'd been in a bad accident when he was young and was disabled. He was my mentor and always encouraged me. And it was kind of his doing that I have this story to tell, though in a round about way.

Well, I loved that bike, even though I could only ride it on weekends after work and had to hide it from my parents. Going for drives alone gave me the freedom I craved, and I spent many happy hours tooling around the countryside while my high-school friends were doing things they shouldn't. I guess I was, too, but in my own way—riding my bike instead of partying.

Anyway, I mention all this so you can get a feel for the kind of person I am, as it plays into the story—independent and stubborn, that's me. I've always owned a motorcycle since then, and I still feel the same when I go riding, free and easy.

So, fast forward a few years—well, about 40, to be exact. I had just turned 56, and I wanted to retire. I'd spent my entire life working as a teacher, and it was getting more and more stressful.

My school district would let you retire after 30 years, and I was qualified, having started working there right out of college. I kind of felt like my life had been put on hold all those years, and I was really looking ahead to when I would be free again.

So, one day, just out of the blue, I went into an RV store and came out the owner of a used Class A RV, a really nice Newmar. It was huge—35 feet long, and it was like a real house on wheels.

Class A's are the ones you see on the road and where you hope the driver had to get a special CDL license to drive it —they're like big buses. And mine was a toy hauler, which meant I could drive my bike right into the rear door and haul it with me.

I was so excited, even though I'd spent a good chunk of my savings on it. That didn't matter, as I would now have a home on wheels and could easily live on my retirement checks. I drove it home, scared to death, and the first thing I did when I got there was get my little dog, Barney, and go hang out in the darn thing the rest of the day. Barney loved it, and I wanted to take off that very day.

I even loaded my Harley-Davidson Heritage Softail Classic into the back. I had a long bucket list that revolved around that bike—to ride the Oregon Coast, part of Route 66, and the Cabot Trail in Nova Scotia, as well as go see the great American West.

I always took Barney with me in his little carrier tied onto the back seat, and I knew he would enjoy RV trips, too. I lived in a small town in British Columbia, and there was a new world beckoning me.

It was a weekend, and I remember spending Sunday evening writing my letter of resignation from the school and emailing it to the principal. It was a good day—until it wasn't, that is.

I still lived in my old hometown, and my Uncle Wally was still my best buddy through all those years. I would go see him all the time and help him out, as he was getting up there in years.

Anyway, the same day I resigned from my job, my brother called to tell me Uncle Wally had just passed away—the very same day. It's almost as if my uncle had known I was getting ready to head out, and he didn't want to be there alone without me.

I felt really guilty about all that for quite some time, as I had called him on Saturday to tell him about my new RV, and he had died the next day, totally out of the blue from a heart attack.

I was devastated. I had actually even hoped to take him with me some, get him away from it all and go see some new country. I loved him as much as my parents, as he had always been there for me and helped me out. It was a sad day for me.

I later eventually came to understand a bit better what had been going on with Uncle Wally's death, and I don't think it had anything to do with me at all. If anything, it had more to do with his living circumstances—which I'll explain here shortly—circumstances I'd known nothing about, and I'd thought I'd been so close to him. He'd never told anyone.

Well, my brother and I went over to his house and started going through his things, and that's when we discovered a letter with a key to his bank box. The letter said his will was in the box, so we went and got it.

Uncle Wally had also been close to my brother, and he left him a nice chunk of money. Neither of us had any idea how he'd managed to save it up like that, but we knew he'd always been frugal.

As for me, I got his house. He even said in the letter that he wanted me to have it so I would always have a place to live. I think he worried about my security, as he knew I had a wild streak and would probably run away some day and do something foolish.

So, there I was with a house. I had been renting all my life, as I never wanted to be tied down, and here I was, ready to roll and suddenly with a new responsibility. Don't get me wrong—I knew where he was coming from and deeply appreciated it, but I just wasn't sure what I would do with a house, especially since I had just bought one— my big RV.

I took a few days off from work to take care of my uncle's funeral and get his affairs settled. I did manage to get a call in to my principal, and she said my retirement was scheduled to start at the end of that school year, which was a couple of months off.

It was now settled, and I would be free, except I wasn't sure what to do with Uncle Wally's house. But my brother was pretty sure I could sell it without much trouble, as it was a nice little place in the country, and Uncle Wally had put in some nice gardens and taken good care of it.

So, after things settled down, I was back at school again, thinking of this new twist on things, but pretty sure I could have everything dealt with by spring, when I would hit the road—me and Barney and the Mothership (which is what I was now calling the big RV) and Old Blue, my bike. I was getting excited and spent a lot of my time looking at maps. There was a whole new world out there calling me.

In the meantime, I needed to get Uncle Wally's house ready for sale, and I had no idea what all that would entail. I was soon to find out it would entail a lot more than I could imagine in my wildest dreams.

I had been kind of putting off going over there and digging in, as my uncle had been a pack rat, plus the memories were going to be hard to deal with, being there in his house and all.

But one Saturday, me and Barney got on the bike (he in his little carrier) and rode over to Uncle Wally's. I couldn't put things off much longer, as I had called a real-estate agent and she was going to come over in a week. I needed to get things going.

Walking in that front door was really hard, and I started crying. My uncle wasn't there to greet me with his, "Hey ya, Sassy, how's it goin'?" I went over to his big old leather couch and just sat there and cried and cried.

I finally got ahold of myself a bit, and it was then that I noticed two things—first, the house had an odd odor to it, and second, Barney was acting like he was scared to death and was trying to climb up my leg.

I picked him up, and he then wanted inside my jacket and kept trying to crawl under it to hide. He's a little fuzzy guy, and I have no idea what breed he is, but when he gets scared, he always wants me to hold him. But this was different, he wanted to hide inside my coat.

I held him close to me and decided I needed to figure out what the smell was. No way anyone would buy a house that smelled like that. It wasn't real strong, but it was definitely odd, kind of like old dirty laundry mixed with the smell of pickles. I figured it was something in the fridge, though my brother told me he and his wife had cleaned it out after Uncle Wally died.

I looked in the fridge, and sure enough, nothing. It wasn't coming from there. I went into the laundry room, and my brother and his wife had already cleaned that up, done the laundry and donated all of our uncle's clothes to charity.

Nothing in the cupboards in the kitchen or his pantry, they'd also cleaned all that out. In fact, they knew I was working long hours, so they'd pretty much cleaned out everything except the furniture and a few odds and ends. They wanted to leave enough so the house would look nice for the market and hopefully sell fast.

I wandered all over that darn house and couldn't figure out where the smell was coming from, until I opened the door to the back porch, then it was obvious. My uncle's house had a closed-in porch that went the full length of the back of the house, and it was filled with old wicker furniture and dusty fishing magazines and stuff like that. It was a cool place, and me and Uncle Wally had spent many hours there drinking iced tea and talking about things.

I wanted to start crying again, but I needed to keep it together and figure out why there was this really weird smell in there. It was pretty gaggy, and there's no way the real-estate agent would try to sell the house with whatever was going on.

The door to the porch had been locked, but the back door out of the porch was just a screen door and had a little hook and no way to lock it. I noticed that the hook was missing, leaving a small screw hole, as if it had been pulled off. This left the screen room open to anyone who wanted to go in there. I stepped out into the back yard, and the smell was gone. It was definitely something in the screen room.

I went back inside and sat down on an old wicker chair and tried to think about what this could be. It wasn't like anything I'd ever smelled before. Little Barney was still scared and wouldn't come out from under my jacket, so I finally set him down and took off my coat, putting it across him.

I got up and wandered around the house for a bit, then decided to go home. I would get some heavy-duty cleaning stuff and come back tomorrow. It had been rough for me to go there, and I wanted to go home and recover a bit.

Well, I didn't go back until it was time to meet the realtor there. I don't know why, but I just couldn't bear to see the old house again. I hoped the odd smell would be gone by then, but I actually didn't care at that point.

I was still really grieving my uncle, and selling the house he'd wanted me to have just felt wrong for some reason. But I had no use for it. I had my own life to live and I wanted to travel in my RV. I didn't want to settle down in a house.

I met the realtor on a Saturday morning, and this time, I left Barney home. The realtor was a nice woman, and we talked as I showed her around the house. She really liked its old woodwork and hardwood floors—it was an old-style bungalow with lots of custom touches, like they did back in the 1940s.

Well, I kind of cringed when we finally went back into the screen room, as I wasn't sure if that smell would still be there or not. I hadn't noticed anything in the house, but when I opened the screen-room door, I wasn't prepared for what I did see.

The smell was almost gone, but instead there was something like I'd never seen. In the middle of the room was a huge pile of small sticks and leaves, and right in the middle of it all was a big smashed-down place where it looked like someone had been sleeping, someone really big. The room was a mess.

We both just stood there in shock. What the heck? I mean, if a homeless person were squatting in my uncle's screen room, you would expect a sleeping bag or something like that, not what appeared to be a nest. I had no idea what to think, nor did the realtor.

Well, I told her I would come back later and clean it all up, then put a good lock on the door. She seemed kind of hesitant to even want to continue, but I needed to sell it, so she agreed to write up the paperwork. I'd go by her office the next day and sign it all.

I promised her it would be cleaned up by then so she could show it, as she already had a couple interested in it. I kind of joked around that it must be some of the neighbor kids playing a prank, but given Barney's reaction the other day, I had my doubts.

I called my brother and he came over with his pickup and tools and we started in. As we dug into the mess, the smell got worse and worse. We dragged everything back into the big trees on the edge of the property, and that's when I found something that made the hair stand up on the back of my neck. I called my brother over to look at it, and he had the same reaction.

There in the mud were a series of huge footprints, footprints with toes and a heel that looked very human, but about three times the size of any human foot I'd ever seen, and also dug way deeper into the mud. The thing must weigh a good three or four times what a large human would weigh, and it gave me the chills to think something that big and obviously bipedal had walked right where we were now standing.

We just stood there a while, then my brother said, "Sass, you need to sell this place real soon. This is too weird, and if word gets out, you'll never be able to sell it."

"Do you suppose Uncle Wally knew about this?" I asked.

"I don't know, but he never would let us kids play back here when we were little, remember? Maybe it's been going on for a while."

This gave me pause, and I remembered that Uncle Wally had never wanted us back here. He always said it was the home of the wild ones and we shouldn't intrude. I had always figured he just said that so he wouldn't worry about us getting lost out in the woods.

"What do you think it is?" I asked.

"Your guess is as good as mine, but whatever it is, it's big. Not something I want to mess with. Drop the price, do whatever it takes to sell it. I don't want to think of you being around here."

Well, that night I couldn't sleep. I even woke up thinking I could smell that awful odor, but it was just a dream. I was nowhere near Uncle Wally's house, and I wasn't sure I wanted to be.

I went back over there the next day and put a good strong lock on the back screen door, though it would still be easy to break in. I had quit taking Barney over there at all, as he just worried himself to death, but I kind of missed having him around as a warning system. I never stayed long.

A few days later, I got a call from the realtor. She said her clients had really liked the house, and the screen room looked great, but why was there a big mess along the back of the house? She thought we'd cleaned out the screen room and put it all back there, but I knew that whatever made the nest in the screen room had built a new one, as we'd taken the stuff way back into the woods out of sight.

Now I was getting both nervous and mad. I wanted to sell the house, and whoever was trashing it up was making me angry, but I was also worried about the whole situation. Something about it was strange—the smell, the size of the nest, the footprints—heck, the fact that there was a nest there in itself was weird.

I went out there and dragged everything into the middle of the back yard and burned it. Since it was spring, the grass hadn't started coming up yet and everything was a bit damp still, but the leaves and sticks that I put into the big pile burned great, almost as if they had a bit of oil on them. It made a big bonfire, and I stayed there well into the evening watching it and making sure it died out.

As I was walking away, I swore I saw something standing in the shadows watching me, something that made my blood chill and triggered my flight instinct. I was quickly on my motorcycle and out of there, feeling like I'd made something or someone very angry and needed to get out of harm's way.

Well, I had another sleepless night, and I was glad I lived far enough from Uncle Wally's house that this threatening person or thing couldn't find me. But I still felt very nervous.

The next day I got another realtor call. She had an offer, and it was a good one. They wanted to buy the house. It took no time at all for me to be at her office signing papers, and it was a done deal, minus an inspection. I wanted to tell them I would drop the price if they would forego the inspection, but I knew that would just make things look suspicious.

The inspection was a week later, and if that went well, the closing would be a week after that. It was a cash deal, so very little could go wrong if the house met their inspection criteria. I knew nothing was wrong, as my brother and his wife had checked everything, and Uncle Wally always kept the house in good order.

The morning of the inspection day, my brother and I went out to the house to make sure all was well. I hadn't been back since the big bonfire, and I told my brother about what I'd seen. This made him nervous, also.

We entered the house with a bit of trepidation, not sure what we would find, but all was well. There was no bad smell, and no more nests anywhere, not even outside. I raked up the charcoal from the bonfire and scattered it in the bushes for fertilizer. All looked fine.

The inspector soon arrived, and it didn't take long for him to go through the house. He told us he would pass it, and we went home, a load off our shoulders. It was looking like Uncle Wally's house would soon be sold, and I would be free to travel.

I had another sleepless night, and I can tell you that being sleep deprived is not a good way to go. I got up the next morning, fed Barney, then made a strong pot of coffee and sat down to think.

What was bothering me so much? The house would be sold soon and I would be free to travel, but I knew I was worried about it falling through because of the weird stuff going on. I decided I would take the Mothership and go park in Uncle Wally's side yard for the next week to make sure nothing happened to the house. My independent attitude was going to make sure this all worked out.

This plan sounded great from the cozy confines of my little apartment, but once I got the RV at Uncle Wally's, things didn't seem so certain. I was feeling the heebie-jeebies again.

I watched Barney, and he seemed OK, so I decided to force myself to relax. I made a hot cup of tea and kicked back on the couch in the RV, and next thing I knew, I was waking up and it was pitch black. I'd slept the whole afternoon and evening, and it was now night. I looked at my watch —it was 2 a.m.

Wow, I'd never done anything like that before, but then, I'd never gone so long without a good night's sleep before. I felt pretty rested, which was nice.

But I needed to feed poor little Barney and take him outside for a bit. I gave him a piece of chicken breast, too tired to make up his kibble and canned food mixture, and he gobbled it down. I was sure he now needed to go out for a little break, so I put his leash on him and opened the door.

I had forgotten how dark it was there, as Uncle Wally lived on the edge of town where there was only one distant streetlight. It gave out just enough light to see where we were, but just barely.

I led Barney over by the edge of the street and he lifted his leg. There was no way I was going anywhere near the bushes and trees, as I was now feeling pretty uncertain and vulnerable. I hoofed it back to the RV and soon was inside with the door locked. I felt like a little kid who was afraid of the dark.

For some reason, I now felt like I should turn off the inside light, as if someone could be watching me, even though the curtains were closed.

I put Barney into bed and pulled his little comforter up over him, and he was soon asleep, his tummy full. He didn't seem a bit worried, and I recalled how scared he'd been around here before, so I decided it was nothing. Barney would let me know if anything was going on.

I peeked out the window and was sure I could see a dark mass over in the trees, but it didn't move, so I decided it had to just be bushes and understory. I finally went back to bed and slept well.

If you've ever experienced spring in British Columbia, you'll know how suddenly and unexpectedly a storm can come through, and sometimes these storms are as bad as or even worse than those in the winter for moisture and winds. And sure enough, I woke to rain drizzling down on the Mothership's roof.

I made some tea and hot oatmeal and tried to wake up. I'd had strange dreams, nothing of any substance, just people and things floating through the air with no rhyme or reason, and it left me feeling kind of off center. Barney must have slept hard, too, as he was off to a slow start and not acting like he wanted outside very badly.

I fed him and then took him for a little walk around the yard, both of us getting wet. I peeked into the window of the screen room, half expecting to see another nest, but all was well. We were soon back in the Mothership, where I dried Barney off and we both warmed back up.

The rain soon turned to snow. I had never really used the RV's heater before and was worried it wouldn't work, but I went outside and turned on the propane and the heater fired right up. We were soon snug and cozy inside.

It was mid-morning when I decided to go inside the house and take a nice hot shower. I then sat down in Uncle Wally's kitchen and started thinking about all the good times my brother and I had experienced there on similar snowy days, listening to Uncle Wally tell us wild stories while drinking hot chocolate and eating cookies. It made me feel very sad, and yet being there in his house was also very comforting. For the first time since he'd died, I was able to enjoy the house and the memories it held without crying my head off.

Barney and I spent all day inside the house, but when it started getting dark I wanted to be back out in the RV, so we went back. It was cold and dreary in there, as the heater had gone out, but I soon had it all warmed up again.

I slept like a baby that night, but at about four a.m, Barney woke me. I thought at first that he needed out, but then I realized he was trying to get under the covers with me and was shivering. Thinking he was cold, I snuggled him down under, but he kept shivering. His ears and nose were warm, so I began to think something was scaring him, and I thought I knew what that something was.

I finally dragged myself out of bed and peeked out the window, and there, up against the house, were two dark forms huddled together in the snow, which was now a good foot deep. I could barely make out from the streetlight what looked to be a large creature and a small one, and they looked pathetic and cold, the large one holding the smaller one up out of the snow.

I was filled with a combination of fear and pity. What were these creatures, and why were they huddled together there against the house? Why didn't they have some kind of shelter? If they weren't able to make a shelter, why weren't their coats sufficient? All wild animals had natural defenses against the weather or they wouldn't survive.

I watched in fascination and fear, worried they would see me, yet unable to tear my eyes away. What were these things? The big one I was sure had to be the same shadow I'd seen before, but I hadn't seen a little one with it.

Now, as the dawn began to light things up better, I watched as the big one tried to open the screen-room door. I knew it could easily break in, but it didn't. Instead, it turned and looked directly my way, and I knew it was aware I was there watching. It gave me the creeps, and my curiosity instantly turned to fear.

It now picked the little one back up and brushed the snow off its coat and began slowly walking back into the trees at the edge of Uncle Wally's house. As the sun began to poke over the mountaintops, I could see its fur better, and it was gray, but not like an animal that was born gray, but more like one that had turned gray, as I could still see places where the hair or fur was still dark.

I could now also see that it was limping, and it seemed to me that it must be very old, as its muscles seemed kind of, well, I can't really describe it, but kind of weak, like an old person's would be. It was like the muscle mass was pretty much gone.

I closed the curtain and sank down into the couch. I knew I had seen my first Sasquatch, a creature I hadn't given much thought before this, and one I had always figured was just a myth.

I spent the entire day in shock, trying to process what I'd seen. Barney didn't want to go outside, so I finally picked him up and carried him out for a few minutes. I didn't want to go outside, either, to be honest.

After a while, I began to worry again. What if the buyers found out the property was Sasquatch territory? Even if the closing went through, could they sue me or somehow negate the deal afterwards? I couldn't say I would blame them one bit.

I started pacing around the RV, which was hard to do in a small space like that. I decided I would move it somewhere else, as I didn't much care for the thought of camping next to a Sasquatch hangout. But it continued to snow, and I had no desire to drive the big rig anywhere, as the roads were snowy and icy.

The day wore on, and I stayed, against my own wishes. I went back inside the house, leaving Barney in the RV, as he didn't want to go out. I went out to the screen room and unlocked the door, pushing it open a bit, though by then the snow was blocking the door. I stood there, looking out through the snow to the trees, then I went back inside, chilled.

I thought of my uncle and how kind-hearted he was, and I wondered if he hadn't known all along there were Sasquatch around. Why else the warning to me and my brother to not go out back into the trees? And knowing Uncle Wally, he had probably fed these creatures and even provided them with shelter. He was so kind that he would even help a creature that could easily kill him.

I then began to wonder if this hadn't had something to do with my uncle having a heart attack. Had the creature come inside the house? No matter how accustomed one got to seeing them, it would still scare the daylights out of you to see one up close.

I went back out to the RV and made dinner. It had stopped snowing and was now getting bitter cold as the storm passed on, leaving clear skies.

Then, on a whim, I put part of my dinner into a container and went inside the house, setting the stew I'd made in the screen room.

That night, I sat and watched, half hidden behind the curtain, and sure enough, what I took to be an old grandma Squatch came limping from the trees. She went straight to the screen room and opened the door. I knew then that she had been watching the house during the day.

She carried the little one inside and didn't come back out. I knew they'd found the stew, and it wouldn't be a lot of food for them, but at least they'd have a bite to eat plus shelter from the bitter cold.

I finally went to bed and slept well, Barney snuggled down under the covers. The next day, I went back inside the house and looked around. Everything was just as I'd left it, except the stew was gone and the screen room had a faint odor in it.

I made a fire in the living room fireplace and just set there half the day, feeding the fire and thinking. I knew Uncle Wally had wanted me to have the house as a security measure so that I would never be homeless. Why had I been so eager to sell it? I knew the answer—I didn't want anything holding me back from my new adventure.

But what if Uncle Wally was right? What if I someday wanted or needed a place to return to? Right now it didn't seem to be a worry, but what if I got sick or injured? Where would I go?

As I sat there by that fire, I began to see my uncle's wisdom in giving me the house instead of cash, like he'd given my brother. I was a fool to sell this place, as it would be impossible for me to replace it. I wasn't getting enough money from it to buy another house this nice, especially in the same town that my family lived in.

I then thought of the old Sasquatch and the young one. Was it her granddaughter or maybe her grandson? What was her story—had the young one's parents been killed somehow?

I began to wonder how it must feel to be so vulnerable, and I decided then and there to not sell the house. My sassy attitude, thinking I could weather anything, might someday become a detriment to me. I could still have my RV adventures and yet also keep the house, as I knew my brother would take care of it for me.

I called the realtor and cancelled the contract. I knew the young couple would be disappointed, but they would find another house, and they would thank me if they knew how close they'd come to living in Sasquatch territory.

My realtor wasn't initially too happy, but when I told her what had been making the nests, she changed her tune. I think she thought I was maybe nuts, but then, what if I weren't? She knew the buyers could come to her and want the deal negated if they found out. It would be a big mess.

I finally told my brother what I was doing, and after thinking about it for a bit, he agreed it was what needed to be done. I think he was happy to know I would be coming back and that now I had the option to return anytime I wanted.

I finally got everything together and was headed out of town. I was going to spend the summer driving all through western Canada, then head into the United States, going south to Arizona for the winter. I was allowed to stay there six months each year, and I was really excited at the thought.

My last stop on my way out was at Uncle Wally's house. I made sure the back screen was unlocked, then I sat an open sack of dog kibble by the back steps. I thought I saw shadows in the bushes, but wasn't sure. I left with a feeling that I had done the right thing, and that Uncle Wally would be happy if he were still alive.

It was months later, in early fall, that I got sick. I was near Ajo, Arizona, almost to the Mexican border, and I came down with a really bad flu virus. I had made friends with some fellow snowbirds who were camping nearby, and they finally came and took me to the hospital in Tucson, where I spent a week. My friends took care of Barney this whole time, thankfully.

When I got out, I was weak and still trying to recover, having a hard time because I'd also managed to contract a pneumonia. I knew it was time to go home.

My brother flew down and drove the Mothership back to Uncle Wally's, where I spent several months recuperating. I was so happy to have a place to go, and it just reaffirmed that I'd made the right decision.

Eventually I was better and ready to give it another shot, ready to hit the road again. One evening, the day before I was going to leave, I sat in the back screen porch, watching the shadows.

While I'd been gone, my brother had been placing sacks of dog kibble behind the house, and the creatures were now coming up every day to eat. I'd continued feeding them while I was there, though they never let me see them.

Maybe they knew I would be leaving, because as I sat there, a small Sasquatch stepped from the bushes and quietly came to where the food was. It picked up the sack and carried it over to a waiting figure in the trees, which I knew had to be the old Squatch.

The old creature stepped out for a moment, then looked my way and made a clicking noise like nothing I'd ever heard before. Somehow I knew it was trying to communicate to me, to tell me thank you.

It wasn't long after, while I was back in the U.S., that my brother called to tell me the Sasquatch had stopped coming to the house. I wondered what had happened to them, but neither of us ever saw them again.

It made me happy to know I had been able to help them, even if just for a while. I knew Uncle Wally would be happy about that, and knowing that made me feel happy also.

And I knew they had helped me make the right decision, though I also knew they had no idea how helpful they'd been to me. Just like it had been for them, Uncle Wally's house was now a refuge for me.

The Karelian Bear Dog

This fellow, Johnny, was quite the character. He was one of the oldest fellows I've ever had on one of my trips, but he was as feisty and hardy as they come—in fact, I wondered why he would even come on a guided trip, as he seemed pretty self-sufficient, and he told me it had been a gift from his grandson.

He still has Nikki, though she's pretty old, so this story didn't happen all that long ago. That means there are still Squatch up in the Yukon, which to me is a good thing. Johnny told this story around a campfire up on the Jefferson River in Montana. — Rusty

My name is Johnny Johansson and I used to live in the Yukon. I spent many years there working as a trapper before I finally had enough of that hard lifestyle and moved to Victoria to stay at my sister's place. I'm now retired, and sometimes I miss being out in the backwoods, but I only have to remember why I left and it makes me happy to be where I am.

People think being a mountain man is a great way to live, and in some ways it is, though it's a hard life. But I can tell you right here and now I'm never going back out there again, and I'll tell you why—there's no sunrise or sunset beautiful enough, no solitude or anything that's enticing enough to ever get me out in those woods again.

I worked as a trapper from the day I was 16 until I left at the age of 63. That's a pretty long time, and I can say I'd pretty much seen it all in terms of wildlife and the crazy things that happen that make you think you're going to die—things like grizzly bears and moose and even a crazed bobcat that tried to kill me, believe it or not. That's quite a story in itself, but that story doesn't hold a candle to the one I'm about to tell you, if I can get going on it.

Anyway, after I had a number of pretty scary run-ins with bears, my sis got me a Karelian Bear Dog. She had to buy the darn thing, and I never would've gone along with that, but she already had it by the time I found out her plan.

These Karelian Bear Dogs, they were bred for hunting and scaring off bears and have virtually no fear. They originally came from Finland and are black and white, sort of a medium-sized dog. You have to keep an eye on them, because they'll flat out tear into another dog and kill them if they don't like them, which is maybe why they're not popular as pets. They have to be fierce to hunt bears.

I'd made the mistake of telling my sis about a few bear encounters, and she took them as being life-threatening enough that it made her worry. She knew a guy who had one of these bear dogs, and one thing led to another, and next thing I knew, Connie was driving up to meet me with this dog.

The last thing I wanted was a dog. Dogs attract bears, and I didn't need more bears around. But I drove down to meet my sis, knowing she meant well and not wanting to hurt her feelings. I knew she worried about me, as I'm her only sibling, and after she told me about these bear dogs, well, I guessed it wouldn't hurt maybe to give it a try.

I pretty much figured it would end up getting itself killed, but I didn't want to tell her that. I knew she had paid a good penny for it and that irritated me, but what can you do?

The dog wasn't real big, kind of along the size of a medium dog but thinner than most, and it had a cute face, kind of longish and very intelligent looking. It was black with white on its face.

Her name was Nikki, and she was a year old. She took right to me, and after a day of hanging around and visiting, Connie had to get back to her job, so we parted ways and I put Nikki in the back of my pickup for the ride back into the wilds.

Well, Connie would have none of that and made me put that dang dog in the cab with me, saying she'd probably jump out of the back. That crazy dog came and sat right next to me and put her little head right on the crook of my elbow. It was kind of funny—as I was driving, the dog's head would move with my arm, but she went right to sleep and didn't even seem to notice.

I really didn't need another mouth to feed, and I figured I'd just end up giving her away, but that silly dog made her way right into a part of me that nobody or nothing's never made their way into before, and I got right dang attached to her real fast.

She was smart as a whip and even seemed to anticipate what I was going to do before I knew I was going to do it. She stayed right by my side—well, after I first thought she was gonna run off, anyway.

See, when I got back to my camp, which was just a big canvas cabin tent, that dog took off. She ran like the wind and just disappeared. I called and called her, but no Nikki. Then I could see her over on the hill across from camp a bit, then she was over on the other hill behind camp, then just all over the place.

I didn't realize it until later, but she was doing a recon of the area, making sure she knew where she was at and seeing how things were situated. I've since talked to other bear-dog owners and they say they all do that same thing.

Well, about when I'd given up on her, she came back into camp. I'd got some dog food on my way back, so I fed her, and she acted like she was starving. Then we went inside the tent and I took a little nap, as the long drive and visit had kind of worn me out. I woke up at dusk, and Nikki was there right by my side. She never again left camp like that, except later, and that was an unusual event that led her away, which I'll get to.

I got up and made a fire and put some hot water on to boil for some hot chocolate that Connie had given me, and then Nikki and I sat around that fire for a bit. It was kind of nice having someone to talk to, though I don't think she understood a word I said, smart as she was.

Me and Nikki quickly got into a routine, and she turned out to be a really good dog. I was kind of hoping to see a bear so I could see how she acted, as Connie had told me these bear dogs will chase bears off.

But on the other hand, I kind of suspected that Nikki would just end up getting herself hurt, so I was glad when the summer was nearly over and we hadn't seen one bear. Usually I would see two or three by then, sometimes more.

The trapping was pretty poor that year, and I was about to give it up and go back to Dawson City, where I would usually spend the winter, making day trips out into the woods as far as the snow would let me, but not typically getting enough furs to make it worth my time. I would usually just hunker down in a little cabin I had there on the edge of town and spend the winter sleeping and visiting friends at the saloons.

It was one of the last days of the season, and the nights were turning cold and the days getting short, when I went out to check my traplines. I had pretty much made up my mind to stay a couple more days then break camp and head out.

I started back to camp when I noticed that Nikki wasn't around. This was the first time she'd done this, and I worried something had happened. I called and called her, but it was almost dark, so I had no choice but to go back to camp and quit looking for her. By than I was so darn attached to that dang dog that this really upset me.

I got back to camp and was building a fire, hoping the light would draw her home, when I heard a ruckus in the willows down by the river. I could hear Nikki barking, and this was followed by a bellow.

It was a bear! I grabbed my rifle and headed down into the bush, even though it was almost dark. Now I could hear something coming my way, and it was big, and I could hear Nikki right behind it, growling and snarling. Oh Lord, I hoped she hadn't been injured, because this sounded like a big bear, one she wouldn't stand a chance with.

Soon, the bear broke into a small clearing, and there was Nikki, chasing it and grabbing onto its rear end, biting for all she was worth. The bear would stop and try to turn around to swipe at her, but she was too fast. I was amazed at what was going on, at how the little dog seemed to have one up on the big bear, and it was a grizzly, too. I almost felt sorry for the bear.

It wasn't until that bear was running that Nikki finally let it go and came over to me, panting and wagging her tail as if she'd been playing with the kids at the merry-go-round.

But before I could even say a word to her, she was gone again, back into the willows, and now she had two cubs on the run. They weren't all that small, either, and she soon had them running after their mom.

I could hear them in the brush, running until the sound faded away, and then Nikki came and sat by me and started licking her paws. I was in shock. How had this little dog managed to separate a big momma bear from her cubs?

I could then see the danger she had saved me from, as that momma might very easily have come after me if Nikki hadn't been there. The bears were close to my camp and momma bears are very protective. I gained a real appreciation for these Karelian Bear Dogs that day, and until then had no idea what a gift my sis had given me.

I decided that night to leave the next day. I would break camp and be out by noon. It was time, as it appeared that the bears were gearing up for hibernation, looking for lots of food and protein to carry them through winter. I really didn't want another encounter, Karelian Bear Dog or not.

Well, that night, things got a bit strange. Many years of trapping in the Yukon, and I'd never had anything happen like what happened that night. And I was glad for Nikki being there, though in all honesty, her presence is probably what caused it all. She sure came out on the short end of things, though thankfully she was all right. But it sure changed my outlook on things, I can tell you that.

I was tired and went right to sleep, but sometime after midnight I woke with a start. I lay there, listening, but heard nothing.

After many years out there, I'd developed an acute sense of differentiating normal night sounds from what are unusual, and something had woke me up. This sound was different. I held my breath so I could hear better, but now all was quiet.

Now Nikki got up from beside me and started pacing a bit. I knew then that she had also heard something, but like me, wasn't sure what to think. If it were a bear, she would've gone after it—or tried, as I had the tent flap closed. She just paced around the tent, back and forth, but very quietly.

My first thought was that the momma bear had come back. Maybe she was mad, or maybe she smelled food, even though I was very careful to keep everything up in a tree bag outside.

I didn't want Nikki running after a bear in the dark, so I clipped her lead onto her collar and held her. We both sat there in the blackness, listening. I then remembered that I'd stupidly left my rifle in the cab of the truck, where I'd reloaded after the bear incident. I never did that, I always kept it with me, but I guess I was just tired.

Let me tell you something about Nikki. These Bear Dogs are famous for their lack of fear, and the man who'd owned her before me had been a hunter. He told my sis that he had a number of hides around his house—deer and moose and bear.

He'd got Nikki as a pup, and the reason he'd sold her was that she had totally chewed up his bear hides. She hadn't touched anything but the bear hides, but had managed to chew them into shreds. They were prized Kodiak bear pelts.

I mention this because as soon as I felt Nikki start to shiver, I knew we weren't dealing with a bear. She just had no fear at all of bears. I wasn't sure we were dealing with anything, as I hadn't heard a sound, but now Nikki was shivering and trying to hide under my camp cot. She was terrified.

What could be scaring her so thoroughly? A moose? They could be very dangerous, but they usually bedded down at night. Besides, moose make lots of noise walking through the woods—you can hear them coming. A mountain lion? Maybe that was it. If so, it wouldn't bother us. I'd never heard of a big cat trying to get into a tent.

There was a half-moon, and now I could see a shadow cross the tent wall behind my cot. It was tall and couldn't possibly be a lion, as it shaded the tent eaves. It was soon gone. Now Nikki pulled from my hand and hid under the cot.

This had to be a bear! Nothing else stood tall like that. It was too big to be another human, though the thought crossed my mind. But Nikki wouldn't be afraid of a human, and why would she be scared of a bear? It didn't make sense, and there I sat, helpless, my gun in my truck.

I can tell you, seeing that shadow was the first time I've ever felt that kind of fear in the wilds. It wasn't the kind of fear you have when you encounter a bear, and I'd had plenty of experience with that. It was a deeper more primal fear, kind of like one might picture humans felt when there were saber-tooth tigers and dire wolves walking the Earth. I felt like I wanted to start shivering along with Nikki.

What I heard next made the hair on my arms stand up, and I actually did start to shiver. It was someone talking, but they had a weird accent I'd never heard before. It sounded like someone said my name, Johnny.

I sat as motionless as a stone, listening. This had to be a human, but it just didn't add up. It was too big, and why was Nikki so scared? In fact, why was I so scared? I'm not a little guy, and I'm not afraid of people, not even when they're skulking around my tent in the dark. But I was definitely terrified.

Now, as I listened, I could hear more clearly what they were saying—it wasn't my name at all, but rather, "Nikki, Nikki, come, Nikki."

For some reason, this made me even more terrified. Whatever it was, it was calling Nikki just as I did, the same inflection and everything, except it was like their mouth couldn't quite pronounce some of the vowels like I do.

I knew then that whatever this was, it wasn't human, and whatever it was, it had been watching us for who knows how long—long enough to be able to mimic my call. I then recalled a few times when Nikki had been skittish and wouldn't leave my side, and now I knew why.

Finally, I could avoid the truth no longer. I recalled the stories I'd heard other woodsmen tell over a few beers down in the bars at Dawson City, stories I was sure they'd made up during the long winter nights to entertain each other.

But now, it seemed like I was myself having an encounter with the creature in their stories—a real live and probably malevolent Sasquatch. I wanted nothing more than to be down at the bar with the guys listening to their stories, not here experiencing a story that I wasn't sure I would stay alive to tell.

Now the shadow fell across the side of the tent where I was huddled, and I could smell a musky odor that reminded me a bit of the scent glands of the beaver I had trapped for years. But the odor was stronger and had a smell that hinted of garbage. Maybe the Sasquatch had been eating someone's trash, but I knew there wasn't another human being within a hundred square miles of me.

I crawled down on my hands and knees, somehow convinced the Squatch could see me through the tent. Nikki was still huddled under my cot, shivering, and I crawled under there with her and just lay there, holding her in my arms. I felt like crying.

I woke the next morning still under the cot. I was stiff and cold, and it took me a while to remember why I was there on the cold floor. It was that the fear returned. How could I have possibly fallen asleep when scared to death like that?

I had a headache, and it somehow seemed like the Squatch had made me go to sleep. It was then I noticed that the tent flap was open and Nikki was gone!

I can't begin to tell you the feeling I had—I knew my little friend had to be dead, and I knew that somehow the Sasquatch had made me sleep, but I had no idea how. And it would take hands to open that flap, to unzip the zipper. Nikki could never have done that.

The first thing I did was go to my truck and get my rifle. I then began to try to track the Squatch. I actually found a trackway going from my camp, after it had circled the tent a few times. The tracks were huge and sank deep into the soft forest detritus, but I saw no dog tracks. But since Nikki was lightweight I figured she probably wouldn't have left tracks anyway.

I was torn between getting the hell out of there and trying to find my dog. I quickly took down the tent and threw it into my truck, not even taking the time to wrap it up. I threw the rest of my stuff in there and was seriously getting ready to leave, but I just couldn't go without Nikki.

Now that my camp was down, I leaned against a rock and caught my breath. I had to find Nikki. I made a lunch and put it into my day pack along with a water bottle, then I grabbed my rifle and started following the trackway. I can tell you right now that was the bravest thing I've ever done in my entire life.

I wanted to call the little dog, but my instinct said not to alert anyone to my presence, so I grimly followed the trackway, looking for some signs of dog tracks, all the while feeling a sense of foreboding like I'd never felt before. If Nikki had been killed by the Sasquatch, I wasn't sure I wanted to know, and yet I had to know where she was.

I had walked for a good hour when I lost the tracks in a field of rocks. I circled around it until I was back in a meadow, where I then found a long track as if something had been dragging along on the ground.

It finally dawned on me that it had to be Nikki's leash dragging, which meant she was still alive, at least at the time she'd been through there. But there were still no dog tracks, which now puzzled me, as there was soft dirt.

Now the leash drag mark converged with Sasquatch tracks, but the foot tracks were under the mark of the dragging leash, as if Nikki had been behind the Sas, following it. I couldn't make sense of anything at that point, but I was beginning to once again feel that sense of terror I'd felt the night before.

I knew by now that I should trust my instincts—the Sasquatch must be nearby—so I hid behind a large tree and stood, watching and listening. All I really wanted to do was run and get out of there, but I stayed, wanting to find Nikki, but afraid to call out for her.

I can typically walk about three miles an hour through fairly rugged country, so I had a good idea about how far back the truck was. I knew if I jogged, I could be back in about a half-hour. I don't know why this thought went through my head, but it was almost as if I knew I was going to have to get back to the truck fast. As I stood there, I even kind of visualized the way back.

I suddenly saw something black come from behind a rock maybe a hundred feet ahead, and my jaw dropped. It was huge! And worse yet, it walked on its back legs and was covered with hair that draped down off its arms.

I couldn't see its face, but I knew what it was, and it was carrying Nikki, the end of her leash dragging behind. I couldn't tell if she was dead or alive, but she was very still.

I was furious, my fear turning into anger at seeing my little friend being carried away from me. I involuntarily called out, "Nikki, come!"

Nikki heard me loud and clear, and my voice must've given her courage, for she instantly jumped down out of the Sasquatch's arms, catching it by surprise. The giant animal tried to reach down and get her, but she suddenly retaliated and grabbed onto its back leg, digging in her teeth and holding on as if she had cornered a bear.

The scream that the Squatch emitted made the forest suddenly go quiet. I will never forget that sound, it was so primal, so loud, and so angry. It kicked its leg back and forth, trying to get rid of the dog, but Nikki held on. I was scared now that the Squatch would hurt her, as it was now trying to reach around and grab her with its huge thick arms.

I called out frantically, "Nikki, come now!"

She let go of the beast's leg and ran towards me. The Squatch now ran swiftly behind her, trying to catch her.

I had the presence of mind to fire the rifle at it, barely missing it, and it stopped suddenly. Nikki was now by my side, and I grabbed her leash, then stood there, wondering what the Squatch would do next. If it rushed me, I could easily put several bullets into it, but I knew my rifle wouldn't kill it in time to stop it.

For a split second I thought it would rush me, but it then turned and disappeared into the forest. I pulled Nikki along and began jogging back to the truck.

By the time I was back to the truck my lungs were burning and I could almost go no further, but I put her into the cab and quickly jumped in behind her, then started up and gunned the truck on back down the forest road as fast as I dared.

Nikki lay there on the bench seat beside me, and after we'd gone a good ten miles or so, I slowed down and kind of examined her for injuries with one hand as I drove with the other. She seemed fine, but the look in her eyes told me she'd been terrified. I had no idea how long she'd been in the possession of the Sasquatch, and I was, in retrospect, surprised I'd managed to catch up to them.

After an hour of driving, I finally came to the main highway. It was so good to be back on pavement, and I couldn't wait to see the buildings of Dawson City come into view. I wanted to be in civilization more than anything else.

When I reached the town, I stopped on the outskirts, pulled over, and began to shake. I couldn't stop shaking, and after a bit, little Nikki came and put her muzzle in my hand. I guess it was her way of saying it's alright and thanks for everything.

After that, I gave up trapping, and like I said, moved to my sister's place near the city. Nikki seemed happy to not have to worry about bears, or worse, Sasquatch. I did tell my sis the story, and I know she believed me. We talked many times about it, wondering why the Squatch took Nikki and what its intentions were.

This happened a few years back, and Nikki and I are both quite happy to grow old far from the wilds of the Yukon. Her muzzle is now white, and I'm getting some gray hair —probably from that incident, if the truth were only known. But why that Sasquatch wanted my little Karelian Bear Dog I will never know.

The Flood

I've fished the very river in this story and had heard about the epic flood, but I'd never met anyone who had actually been there on that fateful night of July 31, 1976.

Hearing this story took me by surprise, as it was a quiet evening by a campfire near the Yampa River in my home stomping grounds near Steamboat Springs, Colorado. It must have been a traumatic enough event just being there, but having a Bigfoot visit you on top of that—well, all I can say is it's one story I won't soon forget. —Rusty

This story isn't long, but if it hadn't taken place, I wouldn't be here to tell it. It's one of those things that leave you wondering if you were in the right place at the right time or in the wrong place at the wrong time. I still scratch my head and wonder how it all came to be.

My girlfriend Liz and I had planned a trip to hike in Rocky Mountain National Park in Colorado. We were both students at a college in Kansas, and after this story took place, we eventually finished school, got married, and bought a restaurant. But at the time, neither of us thought we would live to see the next day, and many other people in the canyon didn't. One hundred and forty three people died that night, and we were very fortunate we weren't part of that number. Five of them were never found.

It was July, and we were both working summer jobs and had taken the afternoon off from work. We knew a spot where we could camp in the canyon down from Estes Park, the nearest town to Rocky Mountain National Park.

We drove and drove, and finally got to the canyon. It was crowded with campers and tourists, and many of the little motels along the highway there were full, but our little spot was empty.

It was at a pull-off right by Big Thompson River, a really sweet camp spot, but you really couldn't tell it was there unless you already knew. That's why it was still empty. It sat right next to some jagged and crumbly cliffs. We put our tent up as far from the rocks as we could, as I get nervous about rockfall.

I wanted to build a fire, but we were exhausted from staying up really late the previous night, so we decided to just hit the hay, even though it wasn't very late, maybe about eight. We needed to get up early the next day and get on up into the park, where we had reserved campsites.

We intended to spend the entire week camping and hiking. It's a beautiful place, and we were excited to be in the mountains.

I recall sitting on a rock and noting how little of the sky one could see, as the canyon cliffs blocked most of the view. But what we could see was spectacular.

Before long, a three-quarter moon rose over the cliff walls, lighting everything up. It was beautiful, but I had no inkling of what was to come, though the gray tendrils of clouds that began floating over the sky should have given me a hint.

We crawled into our tent and were soon asleep. It was nice and cool and good sleeping weather. Last thing I noticed before crawling in was that the sky was getting cloudier.

I hadn't been asleep very long when I remember thinking I was having a nightmare. I then decided it was Liz who was having a nightmare, as I could hear someone talking. I finally woke up and looked at my watch—it was only 8:45. I had been asleep less than an hour. A light rain was falling, and Liz was fast asleep.

I lay there for a while, listening to the rain on the tent and wondering what had awakened me, when I heard the creepiest sound I've ever heard in my life. It was a siren far in the distance, but you could tell it was being made by something alive, some person or creature, not a mechanical thing. It's hard to describe, but it was just like something with really big lungs imitating an old air-raid siren like in the movies.

I just lay there, listening, thinking I was dreaming, as it kept getting closer. I finally started to panic a bit and woke Liz up. She lay there awhile also, trying to figure out what was going on, then she set up in her sleeping bag.

"I'm getting in the car," she said. "This is weird."

"I'm right behind you," I answered.

We both stumbled from the tent and jumped into the nearby car, where I locked the doors and put the key in the ignition, ready to take off. I really didn't want to leave our tent and gear there, but I was ready to do whatever was necessary if this noise got any closer.

We both just sat there, the windows opened a crack, listening and trying to understand what we were hearing. The siren echoed and echoed across one side of the canyon and then back across the other, and as it got closer, I was amazed at how loud it was. It was truly surreal.

Because we were in a place in the canyon where there weren't any motels or other campsites, we had no idea if anyone else could hear it or not. Where we were was pretty secluded.

The siren sound was now really loud and sounded like it was very close. I freaked out and started up the car just as Liz started shouting something like, "Oh my god look at that." I looked up just in time to see a huge set of glowing eyes right in front of the car, and these eyes were a good seven feet off the ground.

Whatever it was, it had stopped making the siren-like sound and was now silent, just standing there in front of the car, glaring at us. There was no way I could go forward, and my reverse was blocked by the tent, with the river right behind that. I just set there in shock, unable to drive away, and this huge creature just stood there, looking at us. Liz started crying, and I myself felt a bit hysterical.

Now, with no warning, this thing began rocking the car up and down. It then started rocking it sideways, and I knew it was just a matter of time before it tipped us completely over. I knew then we would be stuck in the car and possibly injured. We had to get out, but there was no way we could with that creature there, as it definitely seemed to have it in for us and acted like it wanted to kill us.

The car was bouncing around and I hit my head on the side window pretty hard, and it started bleeding. Liz grabbed onto me and pulled me out the side door, screaming and running, dragging me along with her.

Now the creature stopped rocking the car and watched us as we started running down the highway. It soon ran along behind us, and just as I thought it would reach out and grab one of us, it ran past us and stopped in front of us, looking really malevolent.

It was huge, and there was enough moonlight through the clouds that I could make out a very heavy creature that appeared to be all muscle. Its head came to a sort of point or crest, and its arms draped down almost to its knees. It just stood there, blocking our path, eyes glowing, like it wanted to kill us.

I was still bleeding, even though I later realized it was just a surface wound, but I was disoriented. Fortunately, Liz was in charge, and she steered me up the side of the cliff.

"Climb! Climb!" she screamed at me, and I can tell you, I did exactly as she said. We could see well enough to get up the cliffs, although it might be more accurate to say it was more like rocky rubble, not sheer cliffs, that we were climbing.

We were soon a good thirty or so feet up, and I turned to see the creature right behind us. Liz also saw it, and we started climbing again, but had now reached an overhang that we couldn't get around. The creature stood there, blocking our way.

We just sort of crumbled into a sitting position, holding each other there in the rain, and I could feel Liz's sides heaving as if she were silently sobbing. All I could do was hold onto her and hope the thing would leave us alone. I picked up a rock and planned to use it if I had to, but the creature just stood there below us.

And now, I could hear a really strange sound, like rocks clattering together, coming from the distance. At first I thought it was a rockslide coming down the cliffs, but as I listened, I could hear that it was below us.

It got louder and louder, and soon it sounded like a maelstrom of rocks and trees slamming together, and it wasn't much longer before I could see below us a raging river where once we'd seen a small and quiet creek.

It was a flash flood, and we found out later that a thunderstorm had become stationary over the canyon high above, dropping over 14 inches of water into the drainage basin of this small creek in less than four hours, turning it into a raging and deadly torrent twenty-feet high. It had barely been raining where we were, so no one had any indication of what was coming.

The creature turned and watched, just as we did, and then it soon bounded past us and on up the cliffs, making no motion to harm us. It was gone in a moment, leaving behind a dream-like memory that neither of us could really even describe, just a huge dark creature in the light rain forcing us up the sides of the canyon in time to save us from death.

Many others died that night, not even having a chance to escape the floodwaters, as the water was upon them before they could react.

Liz and I sat on the cliffs all night in shock, then as morning came, we slowly climbed back down to the edge of the debris where the raging torrent had now become once again a small river, now choked with huge boulders and dead trees brought down with the flood waters.

Our car and tent and gear were nowhere to be seen. It wasn't until afternoon that we were rescued by a group of searchers scouring the riverway for survivors.

We went to a shelter and called home, and Liz's parents came and got us. We were exhausted and in shock and slept for most of the long ride home. When asked how we woke and knew to climb the cliffs, we just said we'd heard a sound and got up. We didn't tell them what the sound was, and they just assumed we'd heard the flood upstream before it reached us.

To this day, neither of us understands what happened that night. It almost seems to us that what we saw was a Bigfoot, that most elusive of creatures, and it also seems like it was trying to run ahead of the flood and warn people of what was coming.

When it got to us, it knew we had to get out of the car or we would die, so it forced us out, then herded us up into the cliffs. There's really no other explanation for it, as once we were safe, it lost interest in us and bounded on upwards and was gone.

Were we truly saved by a Bigfoot or was it just a coincidence? I can't answer that question, but I am grateful that it took an interest in us, though at the time, I was terrified and sure it wanted to kill us. But without it, we would both have died that night, I am sure of that.

The Woody Creek Monster

I was invited to a campout to celebrate a friend's 50th birthday when I heard this story. We weren't fishing, but just hanging around in a beautiful clearing high on the Uncompahgre Plateau in western Colorado, eating and talking and drinking beer. There was a bunch of us, all friends from way back in high school. My friend had invited his cousin Ted, who made it a very memorable evening with the following story. —Rusty

I'm Ted, and I have an interesting story about something I didn't even know existed until I moved to western Kansas to build a house.

I'm a retired airplane mechanic, and after saving and being frugal all my life, when I retired I decided I wanted to settle down and have a nice place, since my profession had required me to travel a lot. I was married once for a few years, but we divorced with no kids.

Anyway, my mom's family is from Kansas, and I had fond associations with that area, so that's where I decided I wanted to live. Land was reasonably priced and it was a good central location for when I wanted to travel, assuming I ever did again.

So, I bought a nice big chunk of land out next to some fallow wheat fields that the farmer was being paid by the government to let sit. That was the kind of neighbor I wanted—nobody.

I bought 160 acres of prairie—part of it had never been farmed because it went through rolling hills along a creek with lots of big trees. I'll call it Woody Creek, though that's not its real name. It was remote and beautiful with lots of deer and other wildlife—wildlife I had no idea even existed until I had a close encounter or two.

But I'm getting ahead of myself here.

I bought a little old travel trailer and pulled it onto the property, paid a small fortune to have an electric line run in, and got started. It was an ambitious project for a retired guy like me, especially since I'd never built a house. But I had done lots of woodwork as a hobby, so I figured I could learn as I went along.

I decided to begin with the garage. That would give me a place to store supplies and tools, and I could also pull my little trailer in there and get out of the elements if I needed to. I'd put a bathroom in the garage, and if worse came to worse and the house took a long time, I'd still have the comforts of home.

I even bought a washer and dryer to put in there. Of course, I didn't tell the zoning people this, as they would've made me jump through lots of hoops. My motto has always been that it's better to ask forgiveness than permission.

So, I pulled my old travel trailer under some of the big trees down by the creek and got to work. It was such a pretty spot that it was hard to make myself do anything but sit around drinking beer and watching the many mule deer that came around. They weren't afraid of me, which was pretty cool, and I figured there hadn't been any hunting in there for years for them to be so tame.

I had to go to the little nearby town for building supplies, as they wouldn't deliver anything until I got the road fixed up better, which I wasn't sure I was ever going to do.

I liked it just like it was, rough and hard to get down, as that would deter people from coming by. I'm not really antisocial as long as everyone leaves me alone.

I had no idea that a place in rural Kansas could be so remote and unvisited. Heck, I'd had more company when I camped out in the backcountry of Idaho, where I'd gone to escape from it all. Nobody vacations in the wheat fields of Kansas, and I liked it that way, in spite of all the heat and humidity.

Things were going along pretty well, and I'd managed to pour a cement foundation for the garage, along with the help of a cement contractor I'd talked into coming out. I had to pay him a little extra, but he managed to get out there. I would need his services again when I built the house, so I didn't mind paying a little more. We poured and finished the concrete pad for the garage in no time.

He was an old timer and seemed interested in what I was doing, plus he had some information about the place that I hadn't known before.

"This is the old Casey Place," he offered as he stuck a wad of chew in his mouth. "Nobody's lived here for a couple of years. See that mound over there? That's where they had their root cellar, all collapsed now."

"Where was the house?" I asked.

"They moved it into town, but I think it sat over there where that old lilac bush is blooming. I think the old lady planted lilacs all around the edge of the house."

I had noticed the bush and wondered where it came from.

"Why did they leave?" I asked.

"I'm not sure, but I think the old man broke his leg and it never healed right, so he had to give up farming. They used to farm that half-section next door. I don't think they ever did any farming on this land here, too hilly and rocky."

"I wonder why they built their house over here and not on the land they were farming? Seems kind of inconvenient."

"Yeah, but this is more protected here and close to the water, and I think they were just renting the land next door. Guess they weren't too worried about the Woody Creek Monster," he said with a knowing look.

"What the heck's that?"

"I didn't figure your realtor mentioned it," the old guy said nonchalantly. "It's all nonsense anyway—ain't no such thing."

"But what is it?"

"It ain't nothin'. You know how people are, they like to scare each other. It's just some big black thing that looks kind of like a half-human half-ape that supposedly follows the creek here. It's been seen all the way from old Joe's place on down into these parts, but that was years ago. Some people say that's why the Caseys left."

I laughed. It seemed to me that the folks in these parts were maybe a bit superstitious.

The old guy continued, "If you look around in this chalky dirt here, you can find sharks' teeth. Kansas was once underneath a big ancient ocean. You might even find the bones of a dinosaur-crocodile thing called a mosasaur. I personally think if there's any such thing as a Woody Creek Monster, it's the descendant of that, not no half-ape half-human nonsense. Well, I gotta git, but you call me when you're ready to do the house foundation."

With that, the old guy pulled himself up into the big cement truck and was gone, leaving me to contemplate what I'd just learned. I kicked around in the dirt a bit, but didn't see any sharks' teeth. I decided it would be something interesting to do if I got bored—go sharks'

teeth hunting. I had never dreamed of finding sharks'
teeth in Kansas.

The days went by quickly, and I needed to get my ducks in
a row on this garage thing so I would have a decent
shelter when winter hit. I was kind of stumbling along
slowly, as construction was a new thing for me and I had
to learn the building codes, but after some time I finally
had the darn thing framed and roofed and had even
finished the plumbing and electrical.

It was coming along pretty good, and it looked halfway
professional. I think I had single-handedly paid the salary
of at least one hardware store employee with all my
purchases, which included a bunch of how-to books.

I was toying with the idea of taking my little trailer and
heading south for the winter rather than sticking to my
original plan of staying there and holing up. I really had
hoped to have the house started by now, but I didn't—the
garage wasn't even finished, and the days were getting
shorter. The idea of holing up in a garage all winter didn't
really appeal to me too much.

It was now autumn, and as the nights got longer and I spent more time in my little trailer, I began to think more about the idea of the Woody Creek Monster. Being all alone probably had something to do with it, too. I'm not at all superstitious nor inclined to believe in such silly things, but a couple of recent incidents had set my mind in that direction.

One night a few weeks earlier I had noticed that the deer were missing. They had always come down to the creek in the evening to drink at this one watering hole where the banks were low, and I enjoyed watching them from my window. But suddenly, just like that, no deer.

I wondered if they hadn't migrated somewhere else for the winter, but it seemed too early. I then wondered if it weren't hunting season and they'd left to save their hides, but I asked in town and it was also too early for that. Besides, why leave when they were perfectly safe at my place?

The missing deer puzzled me, but I just figured it was natural, and they were hanging out somewhere else. But then, about a week after that, I was sitting one evening in my camp chair drinking a beer when I heard a sound way off in the distance. It was like nothing I'd ever heard, and it made my skin crawl.

It made me think of the old cement truck driver's mosasaur, whatever the heck that was. But it did sound a bit like a crocodile, in that the roar ended in a sort of gurgling noise, though it actually sounded more like a big gorilla. I'd heard a gorilla once at a zoo, but this was way louder and deeper.

Well, this gave me pause, because I recalled what the cement contractor said about the half-ape half-man thing, and it bothered me so much that I decided to pull my trailer into the garage the next day, just for added security.

I got plenty irritated at the old guy for planting the seed of fear in me, though I knew I really didn't have to go there —it was my choice. But what the heck was that sound? I finally decided it must be a rutting elk or something, even though I didn't know if Kansas even had elk. I was beginning to feel more and more exposed and vulnerable out there all by myself.

Well, the next day I got busy and kind of forgot all about the noise and also forgot to put my trailer in the garage. Actually, I didn't really forget, I just decided I was being silly. I had some more work to do inside, and having the trailer in there would just get in my way.

That evening, as the sun was setting, I was cooking some hamburgers on my grill when I thought I saw something in the shadows over by the lilac bush where the old house had been. I was hoping the deer were back, but it was too dark in color to be a deer, so I wasn't sure what it was. Maybe it was that elk. I couldn't see much, just a big shadow.

I had dinner, then kicked back and smoked my pipe for a bit, glancing back over toward the lilac in case that elk came back, then decided I'd go to bed. I'd put in a good day's work, and that darn garage was finally about done. I was feeling pretty good about that.

Now, I know what you're thinking. If you've heard or read any good Bigfoot stories, this is where things are supposed to get interesting. You hear a noise, and that sets you up for the action, then you actually see something and things get weird and scary.

I know this now because after all this happened, I was at my son's place down in Texas, and I read a bunch of those stories on the internet. I'd never even really given Bigfoot much thought until all this happened.

But nothing unusual happened that night. I went to bed and slept like a baby. In fact, I slept a little too hard. I woke up the next morning kind of groggy and disoriented. I thought maybe I was coming down with a cold or a sinus infection, to tell the truth, but after I got up and moved around some, I was fine.

I spent that day installing drywall, and then around evening, I decided to just make tuna sandwiches for dinner, as I wasn't in the mood to cook. I didn't really mind the cooking so much—it was the cleaning up afterwards that I didn't want to do.

So, I sat there, finished my sandwich, then pulled out my pipe. I decided I'd forego the beer after not feeling so great that morning, though I'd only had two beers with my hamburger that previous evening.

Sometimes, I like to get out my harmonica and play. I'm not very good, but I enjoy it, though it's not something I do when there are people around—another reason I liked living in the boonies.

OK, I was sitting there playing the mouth harp when I thought I saw something dark over in the trees, and this time I could make it out a bit better. It was tall, and it looked pretty big. I wondered if my playing hadn't attracted it.

I immediately went inside my trailer. I have to admit it scared me, and I wished I'd pulled my trailer into the garage like I'd planned on doing.

I set there for a while, then decided to heck with it, I was going to move the trailer in right then and there. No point in worrying all night. So I got out, started up my truck, hooked the trailer up and backed it into the garage. I then unhooked it and pulled my truck in next to it and closed the big garage door.

I felt much better, and, I'll admit, safer, though I had no idea what I would be safer from. But what that guy had said about the Woody Creek Monster had kind of stuck with me, and a chill ran down my back.

I puttered around in the garage for a bit, nervous, then decided to go to bed. I shut off the lights and went and looked nervously out the back window of the building.

There it was, that big dark shadow again, and it was right over by the lilac bush, not even trying to hide. I guess since it was almost dark, whatever it was felt secure.

I ran and got my binoculars from my truck, but it was too dark to really see, and all I could make out was something big and black, standing on two thick legs.

I watched it, feeling a bit safer inside, but also kind of amazed at how big it was and knowing it could easily get into my garage if it wanted. And I can tell you, I didn't like that thought one bit.

As I watched, it walked around in circles near the lilacs, kind of like it was walking around where the house had been. It would stop and pause, then start kicking at the ground with what looked like really big muscular legs.

It finally went over to the collapsed root cellar and started digging around, as if trying to see if there was anything in it. I could barely see what it was doing in the fading light, but it excavated that caved-in cellar in just a few minutes. I can tell you this gave me pause, as it had to be pretty powerful to do that. I really began to worry and didn't feel one bit safe.

It turned and looked over at the garage and started making a moaning sound, like it was about to die. It was really mournful sounding, like someone who was just beside themselves with grief. It was almost a sobbing sound, but it then turned into that gurgling again, and the hair on the back of my neck stood on end.

I had no idea what was going on, but it made me wonder if maybe it wasn't crying out for what had once been there. Had the Casey family known this thing? Did they somehow have a relationship with it and had left it there, with it not knowing where or why they'd gone? Maybe they had been feeding it, I thought.

It was really creepy, I can tell you that. I don't own a gun, but I was beginning to wish I had one, because I can tell you I didn't feel a bit secure now, even in that garage. I even toyed with the thought of going into town for the night, but my curiosity kept me glued to the window, watching that thing, and I was actually too scared to open the garage door to drive outside and leave.

It made this moaning sound, then it started ripping things up. It tore up that pretty little lilac bush—I confirmed that the next day. It also went back to the root cellar and tore the heck out of the few old wood posts there, throwing them into the creek.

Well, it didn't take long until it came over to the garage. I saw it coming, and I wasn't sure what to do, and as it got closer I could see its eyes shining this unearthly green. I panicked and got into my truck, the garage door opener in my hand, ready to make a break if need be.

I sat there with the truck window down so I could hear what was going on, and things got very quiet. I had at first heard it storming its way over to me, but now there was no noise of any kind, and this really bothered me, as I had no idea where it had gone. I could feel my heart beating in my chest as the adrenaline kicked in.

I just sat there, terrified. I was scared because I could now hear it trying to get into the garage, and it sounded like it was taking the building apart, stick by stick.

It first sounded like it was ripping off the window trim, then the outside boards. I wondered why it didn't just break out the glass to get in, but I later decided it didn't know what glass was and that it was breakable.

I didn't know what to do. I was ready to flee, but the thought of this thing tearing down all my hard work just didn't set well with me, in spite of my terror. Sure, I was scared to death, but I couldn't just sit by and let this crazy creature tear everything down.

I started honking the horn, long and loud. I honked it so long I was afraid I was going to run the battery down, so I finally stopped. I then sat there, and all was quiet.

I was afraid to get out and go look out the window again, so I just sat there in the truck with the doors locked. I must've gone to sleep, because I finally looked up and I could see light outside, and I realized it was almost dawn.

I sat there until it was about seven a.m. before I got up the courage to go look out the window. I then went all around the garage, looking out the windows. It appeared the thing was gone, so I pressed the garage door button and drove my truck outside. No way was I going to go outside without some kind of protection.

I saw nothing, and I finally drove over by where the house had stood. That's when I saw the destruction, and whatever had done it was very strong and powerful. It would've made a good construction partner if you could harness it, I recall thinking wryly.

I also found huge tracks, which didn't surprise me one bit, based on how big the thing had looked in the shadows. It had to have been really large, as it took two of my footprints to make up one if its.

I then went back to the garage and looked around. The damage wasn't too bad, but it had to have big strong hands to do what it did, ripping off several big two-by-six boards that I had attached securely with 3 1/2 inch decking screws.

I drove back inside and closed the door. I then got out and went into my trailer, then just sat there and thought for the longest time.

I decided it was time to go. Sure, I was scared, but I knew whatever it was, I had no chance against it without some kind of powerful weapon. I really didn't want to spend the winter there anyway, and the entire place now had a bleak and empty feeling to it.

It's hard to describe, but it all felt very forlorn now, not some place I wanted to be, desolate. Maybe it was the beast's cry that lingered with me, and I had to get out of there. Hearing that creature in torment and anguish over some loss really messed with me.

I put all my tools away in the garage, then I sorted out things in my trailer, readying it for travel. This took a good part of the day, but I was ready to leave by about three, which was pushing it. I didn't want to even be there anymore, yet alone along towards evening.

I didn't know where I was going, but I figured maybe I'd go spend a couple of weeks with my kids in Texas.

As I drove away, I thought of how my feelings contrasted with those when I'd arrived that spring. I was all excited and happy to have a nice place like this to call home, and now I just felt lonely and desolate—lost and traumatized.

I had a couple of tools I'd rented from the local hardware store, so I stopped in town to drop them off and to say goodbye to a couple of the guys who worked there and had become friends of a sort.

They asked about my leaving, and I tried to be vague, but one of the guys, Ralph, followed me out to my truck, where he asked if I wanted him to go out there and check on the place once in a while. To my surprise, I answered no, telling him I'd decided to sell it.

This was straight from my gut, and I hadn't even really thought about it, but getting away from there made me realize I didn't want to go back.

I told Ralph to go get my tools and he could have them, telling him how to get in with a hidden key. I was going to stop by a realtor on my way out of town and sign whatever papers I needed to list it.

Ralph stood there for a minute, chewing on the end of an unlit cigarette, then said, "That Woody Creek guy won't hurt you. He's been out there for a good forty years or more and never hurt nobody."

"It's not some guy, Ralph," I replied. "It's not human."

"I know that," Ralph answered. "Everyone around here knows it's a Bigfoot. Old Man Casey, he used to feed it, until he had to abandon the place. You should go talk to him. He'll tell you it won't hurt you."

I told Ralph about how the monster had acted like it was mad because the house and everyone were gone, and Ralph said he was going to tell Mr. Casey about that, as he'd felt bad about leaving the beast and moving into town after feeding it for so many years.

Well, you can imagine how all this made me feel—it was bad enough to have seen this thing, but to be there at the hardware store parking lot and talking about it like it was someone's abandoned dog, well, it just seemed unreal.

I said goodbye to Ralph and headed for the realtor's office, where I immediately listed the property for what I'd paid.

To heck with the cost that went into the garage, I just wanted to sell it. If I could get my money back out of it, I would chalk it up to experience and buy something right in the middle of some little comfortable town somewhere.

I was in Texas when the property sold. I took a bit of a loss, but I was glad to be rid of it. It wasn't long afterwards that Ralph called me and told me he'd got the tools, thanking me.

He then added, "Rumor has it that Old Man Casey's moving back onto the place. He's going to live in your garage and plant a garden and try a small orchard."

"No kidding?" I replied. I was surprised, as Mr. Casey's name wasn't on the contract I'd signed.

"Yup. His kids bought it for him. His daughter is the wife of the James O'Riley you sold it to. He's a banker here. They bought it for the old guy to retire and live out his years."

"Well, Ralph," I replied, "I hope he has many more good years in him. But he won't if he scares easily."

Ralph laughed, then added, "Come on back out sometime and visit. We'll go find some sharks' teeth."

I told him I would, though we both knew better.

As I hung up the phone, I felt a sense of relief. I guess I felt kind of glad that the Woody Creek Monster would no longer be alone and hungry and so forlorn, as strange as that may sound.

And to this day, if I'm feeling sad about something, I just think of the sadness and desolation of that Bigfoot's moan, and everything seems better in comparison.

All that Sparkles is Not Gold

I was more than surprised to have this guy join one of my fishing expeditions, as I rarely get people who are professional outdoorsmen, like he was. They usually just guide themselves wherever they want to go. But he said he wanted to learn flyfishing from a pro, which I guess makes sense.

But I was also surprised to hear his story, as I know a lot of government rangers avoid the topic of Bigfoot. My theory is they don't want to deal with the prejudices they might experience if they talk about it, though I do know they'll talk about it among themselves—and he's not the first ranger who's told me they've seen one. —Rusty

I'm a ranger with the federal government in the state of Washington, specifically, the western part of the state. I would rather not say exactly where, as this story would get me fired, in all likelihood.

I will go on the record (anonymously) and say that the majority of my colleagues believe in Bigfoot, and those that don't eventually will, as they are bound to have an encounter with one the longer they're in the field.

That seems to be how it is—the new employees are skeptical and the long-term ones aren't. Not that we talk about it much. Nobody wants to admit that Bigfoot is out there because nobody really knows how to deal with the situation.

So, when I was out one sunny summer day and saw what I saw, I can't say I was surprised, and it wasn't my first sighting. But this one was definitely unique, I will say that. I'm not too worried about anyone identifying me through this story because this is the first time I've told it.

Anyway, on with the story. I was on patrol on a pretty untraveled back road. I didn't patrol it much because hardly anyone went there. As I drove slowly along, through the bottom of a deep, wide valley in the thick timber, I caught a glimpse of something shining over on the hillside. It was only a glimpse because the timber was so thick, and it was immediately hidden from view again.

I stopped and backed up a bit until I got to the exact spot where I could see it again through the trees. Something was definitely catching the sun, and about the only thing in the forest that would do that is either glass or something metal, like a rifle.

We'd been having some trouble with deer poachers in that area, and we'd been watching out for them. I thought maybe there was someone back in the dense trees deer hunting out of season. I quickly killed my engine so they wouldn't hear me.

I got my high-powered binoculars out and scanned, and it didn't take long to find the shiny spot. And, sure enough, there was movement there. I was pretty sure I'd caught someone poaching.

Now, they were a ways off, and it eventually dawned on me as I stood there glassing them that this had to be a big guy. And he was also dressed in camouflage, because he blended into the understory and trees pretty well. It looked like he was wearing a work suit, one of those big heavy sets of coveralls.

I stood there motionless, watching whoever it was over there. I could see pretty well, as they were well within the range of my binocs, as long as I stayed where I was.

I watched as this big guy, all in brown, repeatedly bent over this shiny spot and looked to be picking something up and examining it. Then he would do it again, then again. It was puzzling, until he turned to face me and I could see what I was dealing with—a Bigfoot, and not a small one, but a pretty big mature one, based on its size.

OK, we don't talk about Bigfoot much, but a few of us have compared stories, and I knew how fast these guys could run. I could feel the blood drain from my face when I saw him looking over my way, and I'm not ashamed to admit I was scared half to death. It was the last thing I'd expected to see.

The bad thing was, I was heading up the road into deeper timber, and I wanted to turn my truck around so I would be headed down the way I came and be able to make a getaway if I needed to. But I knew if I started up the truck, this Bigfoot would run off, assuming he didn't come after me, and I wanted to observe him some more, even though I was scared. I'd seen them before, but always just a fleeting glimpse, as they were very people shy.

I decided to stay where I was and watch for a while. If he rushed me, I would drive like crazy up the road until I lost him, then eventually turn around. The road went a ways, then turned into a really rough timber road a few miles on up.

The creature finally turned back to what he was doing, picking something up and examining it. I could see that whatever he was picking up was shiny, and it seemed to come from a pile or something, because the things he picked up seemed small. It was just puzzling as heck, because the shiny stuff looked like copper or gold, and it was reflecting the sun's rays through the trees.

Now the Bigfoot stood up full height and again turned towards me. I felt the hair on my arms stand up, and I knew he had definitely spotted me. He paused, then reached down and grabbed something form the shiny pile, then turned and began walking at a fast pace up into the timber away from me. He disappeared from sight in mere seconds, as the trees were so thick.

I wondered if he was going to circle around and try to surprise me, so I drove up the road a ways and found a place to turn around, beating it out of there. But on the way back, I looked again and could still see that shiny place on the hillside. Before I left, I hung out the window and tied a piece of red flagging around a tree, marking where you could see the shiny thing from the road. I got a good GPS reading on it as well.

As I was doing this—and it took only a second—I swear I heard a gunshot coming exactly from where the Bigfoot had walked up the side of the valley. It wasn't that far away, and I wondered if maybe a poacher had run into it.

I went on back down the road as fast as I could without endangering myself, and I was soon back to a campground. I stopped and talked to another ranger there. I asked if anything unusual had happened there lately, and she looked at me kind of oddly and said no.

I then told her I'd spotted a strange creature up the road that was probably a bear, but I couldn't really tell, so to be on the lookout. She knew exactly what I was talking about. Like I said, most of the rangers believe in Bigfoot, even though it is kind of a taboo topic.

I got on the radio and told my boss I'd heard a gunshot, but I didn't want to go back up in there alone. It was getting late, and he said to come on back and he'd get a couple of backcountry rangers to go on out there. I wanted to tell him what I'd seen, but I was afraid to compromise my job.

Management had no time for Bigfoot stories, and even though I knew some of them believed, they were still pretty much denying it at the management level. I think they all dread the day that Bigfoot is proved real, as they'll have a land-management nightmare on their hands.

I went on back to the office and called it a day, going home to dinner and then out to a basketball game to watch my son play. He was in high school and was pretty good and eventually even got a basketball scholarship to a small college.

But I'm getting sidetracked. That whole incident had left me wondering what was going on, and I really badly wanted to go back up there and see what that shiny thing was. Yet I was too scared to go alone, so I let it be. I later talked to the backcountry rangers, and they told me they hadn't seen anyone up there, no vehicles or anything, so the gunshot just added to the mystery. They hadn't found the shiny pile.

Then one day, I was riding along with an employee from a sister agency who was going to a small lake on up that same road to take some water samples. Because we'd still been getting some reports of poachers, I was asked to ride along with this guy just in case there were any problems.

We were now riding double when we went into this section of forest, just in case we came upon something and needed backup, as the poaching had continued. It seems whoever it was would just take the deer's organs and leave the rest, which was very odd.

We got to the place where the flagging was, and I asked him to stop. It was about the same time of day as before, and sure enough, the shiny thing was still over there. I wondered if I should tell him about the creature I saw, but I finally decided not to, as I wasn't sure what his stance on the subject might be. Instead, I told him I wanted to go check out what was shining over there. He agreed to hike over with me.

I can tell you I was plenty nervous, even though it was a bright sunny day and the forest seemed totally normal. We had a kind of hard go of it, as we had to fight our way through the underbrush and downed trees, but we finally got to where the shiny thing was—or, I should say, shiny things.

It was a pile of ammunition, and a pretty good sized pile at that. It was all .22 long rifle shells, some still in the boxes, although the cardboard had mostly disintegrated in the sun and rain. The copper casings were what I'd seen shining in the sun, and the Bigfoot had been picking up the bullets and examining them.

You could tell they'd been there a long time, as they had a weathered patina on them. When I later did a check on the age of the boxes, it turned out that the ammo must have been there over 20 years.

I decided to take it all back to the office, so my colleague and I collected it and put it in our packs. I quickly got a GPS reading, then we headed down the hill and back to the truck. I swear I was looking over my shoulder the whole way back, nervous as heck, although the guy with me didn't seem to notice.

I was really glad to be back inside the relative safety of the truck. We then went on up to the lake, where we stayed for an hour or so, then went on back to the office. I was happy to be back in civilization.

No one had any idea why over several hundred rounds of ammo would have been dumped on that rugged hillside, though my boss speculated that someone had maybe accidentally lost it while out hunting years ago, maybe out of a horse pannier or something. A couple of other rangers actually went back out there and looked around for quite a while to see if they could find a gun, but they never found one.

They did find a place where there were several empty casings of the same ammo, as if someone had discharged a gun there. A closer examination showed that the casings had been smashed against a rock.

I will never know what happened—did the Bigfoot somehow manage to set off some bullets? Was it intentional? I suspect it wasn't, and I wonder if the animal injured itself.

In any case, the poaching immediately stopped. I've often wished I had more nerve, as I would go up there and see if there were perhaps a Bigfoot body around, though it would be a skeleton by now.

But maybe some things are better left alone.

The Dark Secret of Mount Olympus

I met Dina when my wife Sarah decided I needed to hire someone to help market my flyfishing business. I'm not much of a businessman, and Dina had some great ideas, most of which I never implemented. I guess I'm happy with things as they are, kind of slow and easy, even though I'm not getting rich.

As Dina and I got to talking, we forgot all about the marketing stuff as she surprised me with the following story. I'm always amazed at how many people have seen Bigfoot or had some kind of encounter. —Rusty

I'm Dina, and my story involves my co-worker at the time, Jeremy, and a third party (who you'll eventually meet, if you're not so lucky) on the slopes of Mount Olympus. No, not the mountain in Greece, but the one in the Wasatch Mountains of Utah, near Salt Lake City. Maybe I should say there was a fourth party—the guy who passed us on the trail and never returned.

Mount Olympus is the mountain you can see from just about anywhere in the Salt Lake area, and it's a very popular hike. You go up a steep trail for almost four miles and gain over 4,000 feet in elevation, and it's easy but hard, if you know what I mean—a nice wide easy trail that's hard on the legs and lungs.

Except in the winter, and then the trail part isn't so easy, as it gets to be hard-packed snow and ice from all the people

—yes, lots of people climb it even in the winter. It's a little over 9,000 feet high and has awesome views, but it's also one of the more avalanche-safe mountains in the area, so is popular year round. People say it has secrets, just like the mountain in Greece, and I now believe them.

Well, for some context, Jeremy and I both worked for a new solar company in the area that specialized in portable solar gear for campers and hikers. We both really believed in the product, and it was also a fun place to work. Jeremy had been there since startup, working in technical support, but I had just been hired on in marketing. This is important because it will explain why we were up on Mount Olympus that day, messing around in subzero weather and freezing our rear ends off.

I was new and enthusiastic and wanted to do a really great job, so I came up with this kind of cool and crazy idea to help sell the product. One of the systems they sold was a small kit where you could carry a a battery and small solar panel that folded up all in a small pack and use it for your laptop, thus having communications and power no matter where you were.

We had people interested in this product, but I wanted to make a bigger deal of it, as I knew I could really increase sales. So I came up with this hair-brained idea.

I was in good shape and liked being outdoors, so this would maybe kill two birds with one stone by getting me outside and also selling lots of stuff. I would climb a mountain every weekend and post a blog entry from the top of it, using solar power.

I would also post lots of photos about the climb and the views and even interview other people who happened to be up there. The company would give away one system to someone who I met on the trail or on the mountain top. I knew this would be interesting, because a lot of college kids from that area like to hike, and they would definitely spread the word.

I picked Jeremy, the guy in technical support, to be my hiking partner, and he was stoked, cause he was going to be paid to hike. How much better does it get? He was going to film the whole thing, which we would also use for marketing.

We wanted to stay in the Wasatch near Salt Lake, at least at first, where there was cell phone service (necessary for the internet) and where there would be people around to talk to.

Unfortunately, it was the heart of December when I came up with this idea, and about the only mountain we felt safe on that time of year was Mount Olympus. We decided to use it as a trial run, then get going again when the snows cleared off, probably in late May or so, or maybe go down into the canyon country where it was dryer for some winter promos.

So, Jeremy and I were all set to do our Mount Olympus promo, and the company advertised it like crazy. Not that climbing the mountain in the winter was that big of a deal, but we tried to make it into one.

To our surprise, it became the biggest sales promo they ever had, and unfortunately (or maybe fortunately) there's no way to duplicate it. I can't really take credit for it, because what happened was pretty much accidental—or maybe coincidental would be a better word.

We got an early start from the trailhead there at the end of Wasatch Avenue and noticed a couple of cars already at the parking lot. That was good—people ahead of us would pack down the light dusting of snow we'd had the night before, and the thought of others on the trail was kind of comforting.

Jeremy got his camera gear ready—he was using the company's video camera with its backpack case. He would stop every so often to tape my ascent, just to give people a feel for where we were going.

It was a beautiful crisp morning, and the recent dusting of snow left sparkles of powder that floated through the air. Jeremy got some footage of that, with the sun breaking through the remnant clouds from the previous night's storm. We had checked with avalanche control, and the mountain hadn't received enough snow to be considered a danger—so they thought, anyway.

Off we went. It took a while to get our second wind, but we were soon doing a steady pace up the trail, except when Jeremy would stop to film me dragging along, trying to catch my breath.

After an hour, I was beginning to realize that my big marketing plan was going to require that I get in much better shape. Sitting in an office chair all day wasn't going to cut it. I wondered how much a gym membership would cost.

The first part of the trail climbed through tall grasses, then gradually entered a juniper forest. After a while, we crossed Tolcats Canyon, which was really cool, but I was beginning to feel tired, and we were nowhere near the top. We now started up the long side of the canyon, climbing up and up.

We carried on and finally came to a ridge with a stand of big Douglas fir trees, all dusted with powder and really beautiful. We had to stop and take more pictures, and I even got out the laptop and gear while Jeremy filmed me pretending to use it.

So far, we hadn't seen anyone else on the trail, though we did see tracks ahead of us. We were near the summit, with about a tenth of a mile to go, but it would be a wicked and tough climb, as we'd reached the summit block and it was now necessary to climb using our hands. Steep and rubbly —and slick.

We paused, kind of putting off going the rest of the way. I was tired and wishing we could just turn back. Just then, a young guy came half-jogging up the trail, all alone. He didn't even stop to talk, just said hello as he went by, then disappeared on up the trail.

I wished I was in that kind of shape. Then, as I stood and hoisted my pack onto my back, I could hear Jeremy saying something, but I couldn't make it out.

I turned to look at him just in time to see movement behind him, something large like a bear coming through the trees, the snow not even beginning to slow it down. It was very fast and was on us before I could even scream. Jeremy was quickly next to me, and I wasn't sure if he wanted to protect me or have me protect him, but I was beginning to think it was the latter, as he stood behind me.

I guess this ended up being a good thing, though I'm not sure I would ever trust him in a tough situation. But this thing, this big dark brown bear-like creature stopped its charge, stood there for a second, then turned and ran on up the ridge.

I will have to say that Jeremy was a quick thinker, because he managed to get a video of me screaming and this thing running through the woods, though by then it was too far off to make out what it was. He just kept filming long after it was gone, and he also managed to get some photos of its footprints in the snow.

OK, I started sobbing, I just couldn't help myself. About then two other hikers came down the trail from the summit and stopped to see what was wrong. I couldn't even talk, and Jeremy just pointed to the tracks in the snow.

He then asked if he could film the couple, and they were so surprised they just nodded their heads yes, and he filmed them looking at the tracks and me crying and them talking about it all.

I almost got the impression they thought it was a hoax or something, but the more they looked at the tracks, the more they seemed to get scared, as this thing had a stride that would be impossible for a human. It was about three feet between its footprints, and the feet were really large.

The tracks went up the ridge in a very steep place that no human could ever go without some kind of climbing gear. By the time they had seen all this, they were scared and ready to go, and so was I.

Jeremy seemed pretty unfazed by it all, and I was beginning to wonder if he hadn't been in on some kind of hoax, but the tracks said otherwise. Besides, I'd seen it myself, and it was too big and too fast to be someone in a suit. There was just no way.

As the couple started down the mountain, I was close behind them, in spite of Jeremy wanting to go ahead to the summit. I just flat out refused. There was no way I was going anywhere but home.

I think we all made record time down the trail, and I was really glad to get into the car at the bottom. Jeremy had the couple sign a release form, giving permission to use the video with them in it, then we all left.

Well, I can say that promo featuring the Bigfoot was a big hit. Our boss congratulated us on having such a clever idea, and he refused to believe we hadn't staged it, so we just went with the flow. All our following promos featured something to do with Bigfoot, and it soon became the company's biggest and most successful marketing promotion. Jeremy and I both got pretty good raises out of the deal.

A year or so after all this, I was on the internet reading about Bigfoot, just trying to get some more marketing ideas, when I came upon a database of Bigfoot sightings in Utah. I was shocked at how many sightings there had been, especially in the Wasatch Mountains. One guy even saw one in the foothills from his office window.

As I read through them, I was surprised to find one for Mount Olympus, and even more interesting is that it was the same day we'd been there. That made my hackles rise and I even stopped breathing for a minute, because the same day we were up there, a hiker turned up missing and was never found.

This took all the fun out of the marketing campaign. It didn't seem to bother Jeremy too much, but it totally freaked me out.

That hiker had been the person who passed us on our way up—I knew this from the description. He was an experienced hiker and had just disappeared. They had sent out a search team, but there was no trace of him anywhere.

Not long after, I got a job with another company, and it all seemed to kind of fade into the distance of my memory.

Well, about six months later, I got a call from Jeremy asking if he could come by my house. I was surprised, as we'd kind of lost touch, but I said sure. He stopped by after work.

He looked terrible—haggard and like he needed sleep. I asked him what was wrong, and he said he hadn't really given the missing hiker much thought, but lately it seemed to have been messing with his sleep, and he was starting to feel restless and freaked out.

We talked about that event on the trail, and he admitted he'd thought it was something I'd cooked up as part of the marketing plan, and it had taken him a long time to believe it wasn't staged, even though he somehow knew it couldn't possibly be human. But it was just a defense he'd adopted.

This explained why it hadn't bothered him and how he'd been able to continue filming. But why was he having such a hard time with coming to grips with it this much later? I wasn't sure I understood that, but I was willing to help him if I could.

He then pulled out his laptop, saying he wanted me to watch a part of the tape he'd edited out and never shown anyone.

I sat down as he started up the video, and it showed me sitting there sobbing, then it panned on up the ridge, following the tracks, then just stopped and focused on a big tree at the top of the ridge. The camera was still, just focused on this tree.

You could hear me still sobbing quietly in the background, then suddenly a scream came from the distance. It was horrible, and it was quickly over. I hadn't heard it because I was crying.

I was shocked. It had to be the guy who had just passed us, the missing hiker.

I didn't know what to say, and it was difficult watching Jeremy break down there in my living room, sobbing just like I had up there on the trail. When he finally stopped, I told him maybe he should consider taking this to the police. He said he would, though he suspected they would just say he was nuts.

That was the last time I saw him, and I don't know if he went to the police or not. I do know that every time after that when one of our Bigfoot ads came on for the solar company, I had to turn the TV off.

I soon left Salt Lake City and moved to St. Louis, where I was quite happy to be far from Mount Olympus and its dark secret.

I Can't Hear You

This story came my way from a fellow who had signed up for a guided trip in Montana. I have a lot of friends in that beautiful state that guide flyfishing trips, and one had broken his arm, so I filled in for him on the Madison River, one of my favorite places. As they say, it was a tough job, but someone had to do it.

We were all sitting around the campfire after a great dutch-oven dinner (featuring peach cobbler for dessert) when I heard his story. —Rusty

My grandpa was a crusty old guy, a real Wisconsin character. He lived in the same cabin he'd been raised in, way up by a lake in the timber, and he left only when my parents finally persuaded him to go live with them.

I have many fond memories of going up to that cabin with my brother to stay with Gramps. We spent part of our summers there—well, until this incident, anyway, then we quit going. After this, my dad would go stay with him some, and he finally persuaded Gramps to move in with us.

Well, Gramps' cabin was old and rustic and had lots of leaks, but Gramps lived there year round, cutting his own wood for winter and growing a big garden, such that you can when you have such a short growing season.

He had water right there in a little stream that came by his place, and he canned his vegetables and dried the meat from the deer he hunted. It was kind of like paradise in some ways, until winter, anyway.

But I was glad when he finally moved in with Mom and Dad. He seemed to be getting frailer and frailer, and the thought of him being alone out in the woods was kind of unsettling—maybe because he wasn't really alone, as you'll see.

This story happened one sunny summer day—well, summer night, actually. My brother and I had been playing poker with Gramps—he loved to play poker—and it was getting pretty late, so we finally hit the hay. As usual, Gramps had won all our change, though he would always let us win it back the next day.

Gramps slept in the little bedroom in the cabin and Jason and I slept on cots in what was the only other room, kind of a combination kitchen and living room.

We'd had a busy day doing what kids do in the woods, and we were tired. We both fell asleep pretty fast and were soon sleeping hard as rocks. I think this happened when I was 14 and Jason was 15. We were what you call Irish cousins, born barely a year apart.

Sometime in the night I woke, not sure why, as I hadn't been dreaming or anything. I just woke from a dead sleep, just like that. I felt really uneasy.

I knew something was wrong. My instincts have always been pretty accurate that way, and I just lay there listening, and the longer I listened, the weirder I felt. But I couldn't hear anything unusual. It was strange, and I finally wondered if I wasn't just imagining things.

I finally drifted back to sleep, only to be awakened again by Jason poking me in the ribs. He was crouched down by my cot, kind of like he was hiding, and he half scared me to death.

"Be quiet, Tommy, don't make a sound. Just get up and sneak over into the corner with me behind the stove. Stay low."

Oh man, this was weird. Why was Jason being so dramatic? It wasn't like him. He never played pranks, so I knew something was up.

I rolled off of the cot and crawled over behind the big pot-bellied wood stove, with Jason right behind me. I tried to make myself small as I crouched down behind it. Jason put his hand on my arm, and I could tell he was shaking. I remembered that I'd woken up earlier, and I knew something strange was going on.

Jason put his hand over my mouth as if he was worried I'd yell or something, then pointed to the little window above the kitchen sink. There, I could see a dark figure, a big head actually, and it was looking right into the cabin.

Jeez, I knew it had to be a bear, but what kind of bear would be bold and curious enough to come right up to the cabin window and look in? And it had to be the quietest bear ever, as it made not even the slightest noise.

"We need to get Gramps up," I said. "He has the rifle."

Gramps always kept his rifle in his bedroom.

"Let's see what it does. Maybe it'll leave," Jason whispered. He then added, "Holy crap! Look at those eyes!"

The bear's eyes were now glowing a greenish-red, just like it had turned on a flashlight, and that light was scanning the room like it was looking for us!

"Crap is right!" I whispered back. "Stay still. That thing's huge!"

We both continued to hide behind the big stove, hoping the bear couldn't see us, and we were now totally terrified.

Soon the head disappeared. We decided to make a break for it and go wake up Gramps. We ran like bats out of hell into the bedroom, where we shook Gramps awake.

The old guy was getting hard of hearing, so we had to shake him awake, otherwise he wouldn't hear a thing. About the only way we could even make him hear us anymore was to yell right at him.

He woke up with a start and set straight up. I think we scared the old guy half to death. But we didn't want to yell at him, so we were in kind of a quandary as to how to tell him what was going on. If we yelled, we knew we would alert the bear as to where we'd gone.

We tried to tell Gramps using a sort of sign language we made up on the spot, but he just sat there half-asleep, looking both alarmed and mystified. He seemed kind of put-out at us for waking him up. Finally, I thought to get some paper and a pen off his dresser, and I wrote him a note, using my pocket flashlight to show him.

"Giant bear window glowing eyes."

Gramps now looked alarmed and got up, pulling on his trousers and getting his gun out of the closet. He loaded it and fearlessly walked out into the living room.

We followed like puppy dogs, scared and with our tails between our legs. Gramps must have wondered if we were really his own grandkids or some kind of impostors, as his kin would never be scared of a bear, glowing eyes or not.

He opened the door and shot into the air several times, then closed the door, walked back into his bedroom, put the gun away, and went back to bed, leaving me and Jason feeling kind of inadequate.

It had been such a simple thing, dealing with this bear, so why hadn't we just taken action and done the same thing and not woken him up? OK, in the future, we'd be more like Gramps instead of hiding behind the stove. We'd go in and get his gun and not wake him up.

But Gramps hadn't actually seen this thing, and maybe he would've been less cavalier if he had. Oh well, we thought, time to go back to bed.

It took me awhile to go back to sleep, and I finally got up and hung a towel over the window. I didn't sleep too well the rest of the night in spite of this, and Jason said he didn't sleep a wink.

Well, the next morning Gramps wanted to know what was going on, so we told him. When we were done, he looked pretty grim, and he led us outside to look around.

The cabin was surrounded by forest, and there were needles and tuft everywhere, so we didn't see any tracks.

But right under the kitchen window the pine needles were pressed down like something heavy had stood there.

Gramps studied it real close, then looked even more grim. He started yelling into the woods like a madman, well, because he was mad.

"You dang Forest People stay away from here! I'll shoot every last one of you!"

OK, this made me and Jason pause. Forest People? Who were they?

I asked, and Gramps muttered something about how they were no good and for us to stay close to the cabin until he could deal with them. We got the feeling this had gone on before.

That night Gramps set with us by the big stove longer than usual. He was in the mood to talk, and he started telling us about the Forest People. Jason and I couldn't believe what we were hearing, and if we hadn't seen the thing in the window ourselves, we would've thought he was pulling our legs.

He told us about when his parents first came out there and built the cabin, and how the Forest People had tried to scare them away. He'd been a little boy, and he was forbidden to ever leave the cabin without an adult. His parents had finally moved the family into town, but they all returned a year later, as they wanted to homestead. By then, the Forest People had torn down the original cabin, and they had to start all over again.

This second time, his dad had lost patience and actually began shooting at the Forest People, though he really didn't want to kill them, just run them off.

Gramps told stories about seeing them in the woods when he got older and was able to go out alone, though he always carried a gun. He didn't think they were dangerous, but it scared him to death when he would see them, as they were big and powerful looking.

As time went by, they came around less and less frequently, until finally they didn't come around at all. It had been years since he'd seen any evidence of them, but he had thought he'd seen one the last time me and Jason were visiting, and he was thinking maybe they were attracted to us since we were kids, and he knew they liked kids.

We just sat there listening, wondering if Gramps hadn't been living in the woods alone too long. But we knew what we'd seen, and at that point, we were pretty much ready to go home—except we didn't want to leave Gramps there alone.

We tried to talk him into coming into town when Mom and Dad were scheduled to come get us, but he just laughed and said we were being silly, that the Forest People wouldn't hurt anybody. Except he wondered if maybe they didn't kidnap kids once in a while, as the lake had a bad reputation, and there'd been a couple of kids go missing there over the years.

We didn't like hearing that one bit. Now we were really ready to go home, but our parents wouldn't come pick us up for another week. We decided we wouldn't go outside unless Gramps was right there with us.

That night, all was quiet, and the towel over the window made me feel better, as I knew nobody could see us now. Jason and I lay there awhile, talking in low voices, with the light out, discussing what Gramps had told us about the Forest People.

I finally drifted off, but only to once again startle awake in the early hours. I looked at the kitchen window, but the towel was still there.

Jason whispered, "Tommy, you awake? Did you hear that?"

"What was it?" I asked.

"There's something messing around outside. Sounds like it's behind the house outside Gramps' bedroom."

I lay still and listened. Something was making a low moaning noise, and it would then bang against the back side of the cabin.

"Gramps can't hear it," I whispered. "And it sounds like it might be trying to get him."

We both rolled off our cots and crawled quietly into Gramps' bedroom. He was snoring like a saw cutting logs, totally oblivious to the racket outside.

Jason crawled over by the dresser where Gramps' rifle stood in the corner. He picked it up, got some ammo from the dresser drawer where Gramps kept it, then carefully loaded the gun. He now walked back into the living room, and I followed. We would deal with this on our own and not wake Gramps up—or so we thought.

I held the door open while Jason stepped out a foot or two and shot the rifle into the air. Neither of us had spent much time around guns, and he wasn't prepared for the recoil, which almost knocked him down. He came stumbling backwards into me, and both of us almost bit the dust, but we managed to stay on our feet.

I slammed the door shut just as I saw something really big and black come around the corner of the cabin. I locked the door, then quickly put a chair up against it, as if that would have any effect at all on stopping an animal that big.

Jason stood there, rifle pointed at the door, and we both held our breath. We were scared to death.

Of course the rifle shot woke Gramps up, and he came into the living room with his skinny bare legs sticking out of his oversized BVDs. He kind of reminded me of a chicken with his potbelly and skinny legs.

He saw Jason with the rifle and immediately figured out what was going on. Now he was mad.

"Are they back?" he asked with a scowl on his face.

Jason nodded his head yes as Gramps took the rifle from him. Gramps then opened the front door and went outside, BVDs and all. I kind of wondered if he wasn't a bit more scary looking at that point than the Forest People were.

We instinctively followed him, though we were both scared to death. Gramps didn't seem a bit scared, and we were now worried about him. I guess we were feeling protective of the old guy, even though he was the one with the gun.

Well, as I went out the door, I realized we were in deep trouble when I heard the lock click behind me. I hadn't really unlocked it, just pulled it open from the inside. I tried the handle, and sure enough, we were locked out.

The old cabin only had two windows, the one above the kitchen sink and a small window in the living room. There was no way any of us would fit through the kitchen window, and Jason might barely fit through the other one, being the smaller of us three.

"Jason, we're locked out," I whispered to my brother. He turned with a panicked look in his eyes and verified what I had told him.

"Crap," he said, immediately going to the living room window and trying it. It was also locked.

Meanwhile, Gramps had gone around the side of the cabin, muttering and looking for something to shoot at. I didn't know whether to follow him and make sure he was OK or try to break into the cabin. Jason was trying to pry the window open, so I decided to follow Gramps.

I was going around the corner of the cabin in the dark following Gramps when I heard the moaning again. It was terrifying, like something from a horror movie, and it sounded like it was right around the corner where Gramps had just gone. And of course it was too dark, so I couldn't see a thing.

I felt my way along the back wall of the cabin, thinking that surely I would catch up to Gramps soon. And sure enough, I did, bumping into him and scaring the bejeebers out of him. He must've jumped three feet in the air, and for a minute I thought I was going to get shot.

And now the moaning was right there, right by where Gramps stood, and he was looking at me, even madder cause I'd scared him. I knew he couldn't hear the sound, and it sounded like it was right behind him.

I yelled at him and pointed behind him, but it was so dark he couldn't even see my hand. Right over Gramps' shoulder were those eyes, those red-green glowing eyes, and they stood way above both me and Gramps. This thing was huge, and it was about to get my grandpa, and I couldn't make him understand what was happening.

I didn't even think about it, I just grabbed the rifle from Gramps and pointed it at the eyes. I hesitated, as I didn't want to kill anything, and just as I paused, Gramps turned and saw it. I pulled the trigger, but I shot purposely wide, and the thing jerked back as if I'd shot it, then disappeared into the darkness.

I knew I hadn't shot it—I couldn't have possibly shot it—but I was worried just the same. I grabbed Gramps' arm and steered him around the front of the cabin, where we were still locked out.

The thing was moaning again off to our left, and now it sounded really angry. It soon began banging on the side of the cabin, but it stayed around back where we couldn't see it. Jason was now crawling through the window, and we were soon all inside.

I just stood there by the big stove, wide eyed and white faced as Gramps started a pot of coffee, cussing and fussing the whole time. He obviously couldn't hear a thing and had no idea what kind of a racket the thing was making.

It was soon dawn, and things now got quiet outside. We collected our wits, Gramps going on and on about the Forest People while drinking coffee. He had said they were harmless, but they sure didn't feel that way to me.

That day, Jason and I walked down the road to the neighbors, who had a phone, and we called Dad. We told him to come and get us, though we couldn't tell him the real reason with the neighbors listening in.

Dad arrived that evening, and we packed up to leave, begging Gramps to come with us. Of course he refused, acting like he was surprised that we were leaving over something so trivial as a Bigfoot terrorizing us.

That was pretty much it for us wanting to go stay at the cabin, and it wasn't long before Gramps finally gave up and moved in with us.

We were glad he had survived it all, and to this day I wonder how many times he'd been terrorized by a Bigfoot and didn't even know it. I guess ignorance is bliss, as they say.

The Bigfoot Wind

A guy named Charlie told this story one evening near the headwaters of the mighty Colorado River at Grand Lake, Colorado. We'd been lake fishing and were all staying in rented cabins, quite the luxury for me. A bit of a wind came up that night, and I can tell you I was very happy to sleep indoors after hearing his story. —Rusty

Sitting around this campfire with the wind gusting like this makes me restless, Rusty. It also reminds me of the only time I ever met a Bigfoot, not that we really met. This isn't really much of a story compared to some, but I'll tell it anyway.

I'm an attorney, and I live in Kentucky with my wife and two sons. I work for the IRS, and it can get pretty stressful, so I used to get away from it all for the weekend and go camping as often as I could.

My wife hates camping, and the kids were old enough that they were too busy to want to hang out with their dad, so I always went alone. Not that I go anymore, mind you.

I had a little thirteen-foot trailer, you know, one of those little fiberglass things that looks like an egg. This one was actually only ten-feet long, as the other three feet was the hitch. It was small but cozy and easy to pull.

I would leave all my stuff in it, then when the weekend came, I'd just hook it up and be on the road in a half-hour or so. It was kind of like a little man cave, and I kept it all stocked up with food and sleeping bags and everything I needed to camp.

I like to fish, and I'd head for a lake not too far away from home and be there pretty quickly. It was a pretty slick deal for me, and I think my wife liked to get rid of me for the weekend so she could relax and do her own thing.

I always checked the weather before I went, but this particular time I didn't care what was coming in, I just needed to get away regardless, as I'd had a very stressful week at work.

We were putting together a case against a doctor who hadn't paid taxes for a number of years, and he'd also just lost his medical license for malpractice. He was going downhill fast, and I felt kind of sorry for the guy, though I didn't know why. Later, I realized he reminded me of my brother, who always had to do everything the hard way. So, I was a bit too close to what was going on.

I was on the road and heading out when it occurred to me that I should go to this lake I'd never been to, one a friend kept mentioning. He said the fishing was great and that there were few people around. I should've known a place with good fishing and few people had something wrong with it, and I found out exactly what that was.

Afterwards, I was afraid to go out anymore, so I ended up regretting going there. But you can't change the past, and I now play golf instead of fishing. I can sleep in my warm safe house each night when I play golf.

Anyway, so I pulled into this little lake area and immediately noticed I was the only one there. I was really happy, thinking I'd have the place all to myself, without really wondering why it was empty.

I gleefully got camp set up, got out my fishing gear, and immediately tried my luck. I figured with nobody else around, the fish would flock to my bait and it would be like shooting fish in a barrel.

Not so. I sat there for a few hours and didn't catch a thing —in fact, I didn't even see a bubble or anything. It was like the lake was asleep or something.

Finally, I put my gear away and started dinner. It was then that I noticed a bit of a breeze coming in. I was thinking this would be nice as it would cool things down, which it did. I spent a very pleasant evening sitting in front of my little trailer drinking hot chocolate.

I finally went to bed, totally happy, in spite of not catching anything, pleased that no one else had shown up, not a soul. In retrospect, I should've realized something was wrong, but at the time, it just seemed like good luck, even though it was actually the opposite.

I woke up the next morning refreshed and happy to be alone, even though I expected people would start arriving any time. After all, it was a Saturday in the middle of prime fishing season.

I fished all around the small lake, and still no one showed up. The breeze from the previous night was beginning to get more serious, with some pretty good gusts, but not enough to really make me worry—I was too busy enjoying myself and not thinking about much of anything.

By noon, I still hadn't caught one fish or even had a bite. What had initially seemed like a bit of bad luck was now becoming kind of weird. I'd never fished anywhere that I didn't even get a bite. I would've thought that maybe the lake was dead from pollution or something if my friend hadn't told me about the great fishing there.

I shook my head, figuring it was just bad luck on my part, then fiddled a bit with some different lures and bait, but still no luck. I spent all afternoon trying different techniques, and I still had no hint of a fish anywhere. I even walked around the shore's edge to see if the water was clear, which indicates good oxygen levels. Everything looked fine, but no fish.

By evening, the wind had really started picking up, and I noted the sky was now overcast. I wished I'd checked the weather, but I still wasn't too worried. I could be out of there in less than an hour, as I could quickly put everything away and hook up if conditions deteriorated. It was early summer, and about all that would come in would be some rain, and it was a good road out.

It was now too windy to sit outside, so I had a sandwich and a beer and sat inside the little trailer. I had looked forward to a nice fish dinner, but that was apparently not going to happen.

I read a book for a while, then stepped outside. The sun was setting, but all I could make out was an orb behind thick gray clouds. All of a sudden everything felt very ominous, but I couldn't figure out why.

As I stood there, I realized the wind had died down completely, and it was so very still it felt like I was in a tomb. I mean, there was no movement of any kind anywhere and absolutely no sound. It was as quiet as could be, and the thick cloud cover and now-deepening twilight made me feel uneasy.

I decided to call my wife, Mary, and see if she could give me a weather report. It was the first time I'd tried to use my phone, and I soon realized there was no cell signal.

Everything just felt so dark and ominous and strange, so I decided to go ahead and hook up and go home. I was no longer enjoying myself, and the fishing had been beyond lousy, so why stay?

I hooked up the little trailer, attaching the sway bar just as the rain moved in. I quickly jumped into my truck as the wind started back up, gusting enough to plaster the rain against the windows on one side of the vehicle while leaving the other side almost dry.

Within minutes, it was so windy that I was afraid to drive. It had gone from being completely still to gusts that felt like they were at least 40 m.p.h. Just like that, bam, a big wind had come in. I'd pulled trailers in the wind before, and it's a white-knuckle experience.

I was glad I'd managed to hook up, as that would provide some stability to the trailer. I decided to stay until the wind died down, even though I knew it would probably mean spending another night there.

I'd once camped in that little trailer in 65 m.p.h. winds, and it wasn't any fun, I can assure you. I knew exactly how fast the wind was blowing that time because I was camped not too far from the airport where the weather station was, and that was what they had said the wind speed was.

That had been an unsettling experience, watching the bushes literally bend over and touch their tops to the ground from the high winds. The trailer rocked and rolled, but I was fine, and the winds eventually died down and all was well, so I now knew I could survive some pretty good gusts—but I was kicking myself for not checking the weather, I can tell you.

So, I decided to wait it all out and just hunker down. I got into the trailer and opened a deck of cards and started playing solitaire, but I soon gave up on that, as the winds seemed to be getting worse and were too distracting.

It was now pitch black outside, and I suddenly felt the temperature quickly drop. I opened the door, and it was almost torn off by the wind before I managed to slam it back shut.

It had gone from a nice balmy summer day to being downright cold. I could tell the barometric pressure was dropping, as I'm susceptible to getting headaches when it drops much, and I could feel one coming on. I was now beginning to think I was in the middle of a very serious storm.

I turned off my inside light, as I didn't want to run my trailer battery down in case I needed to turn on the heater, as the battery would be needed to run the blower. I couldn't believe it—one minute I'd been enjoying the fishing, and now I was worrying about freezing to death. Well, maybe not actually freezing, but getting cold.

I crawled into my sleeping bag, clothes and all. I wanted to be ready to make a break if the wind died down. I knew I probably wouldn't be able to sleep, as the little trailer was now rocking pretty good. I estimated the winds to be at around 45 or 50 m.p.h.

I must've gone to sleep in spite of it all, as I woke and looked at my watch to see it was around 2 a.m. The trailer was rocking so hard it felt like it was going to be airborne any minute. As I realized what was going on, I contemplated making a run for my pickup, where I knew I would be safer, as it weighed 5,000 pounds to my trailer's 1,000.

I knew the winds had to be over 65 m.p.h., as the trailer felt much tippier than when I'd been in that previous storm. I was now scared to death and actually wondering if I might be killed. I needed to get to the truck, but I was afraid to make a run for it in those high winds. I estimated it was blowing at least 70, maybe higher, and I worried the wind would wrench the trailer door off if I opened it.

It was now really cold, and I put on my coat. I knew the wind chill was making the temperature drop. I turned on the heater, but nothing happened, then I realized I'd forgotten to turn on the propane bottle. There was no way I was now going to go outside to do that.

But now I could hear someone driving up to the trailer! It sounded like an ATV or dirt bike, and I was amazed that anyone would be out in this wind on such a vehicle. Had a ranger seen me and was coming to check on me?

I waited for them to stop, but they didn't—the sound just kept getting louder and louder until it sounded like they would run right over me, and it was then that I realized it was the wind. It was intensifying and howling like a banshee from hell.

I can tell you that right then and there I began praying, and I'm not a religious guy at all. I wanted to cry, but instead, I prayed.

The buzzing noise soon turned into a howling, and I swore there was some great creature outside wailing and carrying on, but I knew it had to be the wind.

I could now feel the trailer actually tip, and it seemed like one of the wheels was up in the air for a moment. I knew I had to get to my truck, but I was afraid I'd be picked up by the wind and blown to who knows where, so I stayed put, even though I fully expected to feel the trailer flip onto its side at any moment. I knew all that was holding it down was the hitch and the sway bar.

Then, from nowhere, something big banged against the side of the trailer, and I knew a huge branch or something had been blown into it. Even though it was fiberglass, I expected to find a hole in it when daylight came and I could see what was going on.

But then, something hit the trailer again, and it felt like it had been slapped by a huge hand. Once again, I could feel the trailer lift up a bit, and I knew one of the wheels had left the ground.

I had been driving in a bad wind once in southern New Mexico, so bad that trucks and RVs had stopped by the side of the road, waiting it out. A coal train had gone by, and the wind was blowing the coal out, leaving a black cloud behind the train.

A big truck had been in front of me, and I had slowed down and got way behind it when I saw one of its rear wheels leave the ground. The driver soon pulled over to wait the storm out.

I knew now how that truck driver must've felt, but there was nothing I could do. I couldn't pull over and wait things out. I was stuck and at the mercy of the wind. The vent in the ceiling was rattling, and I could feel the cold air seeping in around the window seals.

Then, all of a sudden, the trailer stopped rocking and was perfectly still. I listened carefully, but the wind was still blowing like before, and nothing had changed. Why had the trailer stopped rocking? It felt like a giant hand was holding it to the ground, stabilizing it.

I peeked out the window on the back side of the trailer, but saw nothing, just the outlines of the tops of the trees where the full moon cast a strange glow through the thick gray clouds.

I then looked out the other side, and saw nothing. I mean, I really saw nothing, no tree outlines or light or anything. It was as if something was leaning against the trailer, blocking the view—something big.

I was puzzled. The trailer had stopped rocking, and the wind was blowing just as hard, and I couldn't see through the windows on the front side—what was going on?

I pulled back the curtain on the door and thought I saw a large figure silhouetted against the trailer in the moonlight, but I couldn't be sure, even though the hair on the nape of my neck stood up in fear.

Not knowing what to do, I lay down on the floor. For some reason, being low seemed the thing to do. I finally fell asleep, exhausted. When I woke, all was still, and a steady drizzle was falling. It was dawn, and the wind had stopped.

I looked out the back of the trailer, and then the front, and there was nothing there. It had to have been my imagination that something had been against the front of the trailer.

I opened the door and walked out. There, hanging off a small piece of twisted aluminum on the window frame was a clump of dark brownish red hair. I carefully lifted it off, knowing then that it hadn't been my imagination, and there had indeed been something large up against the trailer.

I wish now I had saved the hair, but all I could think of at the time was to get out of there. I somehow knew the thing was still around, and I just wanted to flee.

I was soon in my truck and on my way home. I didn't slow down a bit until I was a good 20 miles down the paved highway, far from that little lake.

Years later, I was watching a Bigfoot show on TV where a couple of guys were playing recordings they'd made of Bigfoot howls. The hair stood up on my neck as I recognized the same sound I'd heard that night and had told myself was the wind.

I think what happened was that a Bigfoot was in the area while I was fishing, even though I was oblivious to it. I had heard of Bigfoot, but never in my wildest dreams thought they would be in Kentucky.

When the big storm came through, I think that same creature sought shelter up against my little trailer, which created a wind block for it. And as it leaned there against my trailer, it also stabilized it enough that the wind no longer shook it and tried to lift it from the ground.

I have no real evidence for this other than the howling I heard, the fact that the trailer quit shaking, and the hair, which was like nothing I'd ever seen, as it was thick and curly. For me, that's evidence enough, and who knows, maybe that Bigfoot kept my trailer from blowing away at the same time it was using it for a windbreak.

In any case, I was glad for the safety I experienced that night, even though I was probably only a few inches from a creature that could have easily killed me and had me for dinner.

Who knows, but maybe it wasn't interested in me because it had already eaten all the fish in that lake.

The Bigfoot Graveyard

There are a lot of people who say if Bigfoot was real we'd find a skeleton. I, too, have often thought it strange that we never have, but maybe they bury their dead, as this story seems to indicate.

Cora is a friend of my cousin, and when I heard she had possibly discovered a Bigfoot graveyard, I persuaded her to tell me the story. I couldn't get her to tell me where it's at, however, because she couldn't remember exactly, as this story took place when she was young.

She did tell me the general vicinity, and I hope to someday get out there and go searching. —Rusty

My name is Cora, and this story happened when I was just a kid, maybe about eight. I had a friend named Karen who was about three years older than me, and she was always getting me in trouble—until after this event, that is, then I quit hanging out with her.

Well, Karen and I had all kinds of adventures, though most were related to the cow pie ambushes we were famous for. We lived on the edge of town and there was a cow pasture next to my house, so that's where we got our ammo. Our cow pie ambushes were famous, and I think kids came from other parts of the little town we lived in just to see if they would be ambushed, though our primary territory was the trail to the swimming hole.

Our aim was pretty accurate, and we eventually even set up a cow pie protection program for kids who wanted to come through the neighborhood to go swim and not get ambushed—the protection fee was usually in the form of candy. If the Mafia had been in our little Oregon town, we would've been early candidates for membership.

I mention this to show you what brats we were, or at least that's what my older sister called us. At the very least, we were pretty fearless and acted like little banshees most of the time. Our fearlessness is what led to this really strange event I'm going to tell you about.

One day, after sitting in ambush for a while with no victims, we got bored and decided to go explore some new territory. So, we went to my house and made some baloney sandwiches, grabbed some cookies and sodas, and headed down the trail to the swimming hole, which was just a place where the creek had cut away at the bank enough that it made a big bend and slowed down and pooled a little.

We had no interest in swimming—it was just a handy starting place for whatever adventure we could come up with for the day. We would sit and eat our lunch there and figure out what to do next.

As we sat there, Karen decided we should go visit this distant hill where we'd seen what looked like an old building of some kind. Of course, distant to a kid of that age isn't the same as distant would be to an adult, so that hill was probably really only about a quarter or half mile away. But to us, it was a long trek because it was unknown territory, and we had to cut through some thick woods to get there.

We talked about what the odds of getting lost would be and decided to use a radio tower on an even more distant hill as a landmark. We sat there like we were getting ready to explore the darks of the Amazon or something. That was part of the adventure, talking about it and building it all up.

We finally finished our lunches and started through the woods. We'd done this sort of thing before, and I'm sure if our parents had known they would've had a fit, but they thought we were at each other's house reading the Hardy Boys or whatever clueless parents think their kids do.

We had set our course pretty carefully, and we gradually got closer to the hill with the old building on it, and finally, with a few new scratches to show for our efforts, we were there.

It wasn't much, just someone's old house that was crumbling into the dirt, long abandoned, the road all overgrown with weeds. A few irises had managed to survive and spread into a small field. It was really pretty, all these deep blue irises everywhere. Karen picked one for her mom and stuck it behind her ear.

So, we looked around a bit, kind of disappointed that our adventure hadn't amounted to much, when Karen decided to climb a big tree behind what was left of the house and see if she could see anything of interest and maybe salvage the day.

As she sat up there, pretty high by my estimation, maybe 10 feet or so (which is pretty high to an eight-year-old), she started making a weird noise like a chicken. I couldn't figure out what she was doing, but I finally gathered that she wanted me to climb up there with her and look at something that had her either really excited or really scared.

I managed to scoot myself up the tree until I was beside her, and that's when I saw what had her all riled up and why she didn't want to call out to me. Not far from where we'd been messing around by the house was an old maroon pickup, and there were two guys standing by it, talking.

We couldn't hear what they were saying, but one of them was holding a shovel in one hand and something big and kind of whitish in the other. It looked like a bone, though we weren't close enough to really tell much, but it had the shape of a big leg bone, like that of a cow or horse or something.

"They look real shady," Karen informed me. I wondered how she could see well enough to tell that, but I usually deferred to her judgement, she being older and, I presumed, wiser.

"Why shady?" I asked.

"They're digging up something bad," she replied. "Let's get closer and see what it is. Maybe we can get some kind of reward or something."

"Reward for what?"

"For turning them in for digging up something bad," she replied with irritation at my apparent slowness. "They're probably crooks, and we can turn them in and get the reward."

I suddenly lost interest in this new adventure. I had no desire to tangle with crooks, and I told her this, but she ignored me. I was soon obediently following her as she crept closer to the two men.

I was amazed at how gutsy she was, but followed along, right up to some shrubs that couldn't have been more than 20 feet from the pair. We crouched there silently, eavesdropping.

"Look, Henry, this is something that we should probably report, don't cha think?"

The speaker was a short stout man who looked to be in his 30s. The other man was taller and older, maybe in his 40s.

Both were unkempt and looked pretty questionable, even to someone of my tender age. The breeze shifted, and the smell of alcohol was strong enough that it made me want to retreat.

"Hobos," I whispered to Karen, and she poked me pretty hard in the ribs, which quieted me right down. Of course, real hoboes don't have vehicles, but I didn't know that at the time.

"Shane, you're a fool and an idjit," said the second and older man. "What I'm holding right here is our ticket to our own rags to riches story."

"How so?" Shane asked.

"This is a wooly mammoth bone, you fool. We'll excavate the whole skeleton and sell it to some collector for millions of dollars."

"Millions of dollars? Who'd pay that for a bunch of old bones?"

"Lots of rich people would, you dummy. They collect stuff like this, fossils and dinosaur bones and all kinds of old things. Build their own private museums to show it all off.

It's kind of like you collect those stupid baseball cards—same idea, but more expensive. We'll come back tomorrow with more tools."

Karen whispered to me, "There's no such thing as wooly mammoths here. It's a mastodon."

I didn't argue, my ribs still being sore from last time she'd poked them. Now the pair put the big bone in the back of the pickup, after wrapping it in an old blanket that looked like it had more holes than blanket. They took off, the truck winding through the tall weeds.

Karen stood up after they were gone and immediately headed for where they'd been. She looked around, me following, then took off in the direction they had to have come from, given the beat-down weeds.

I was beginning to get a real creepy feeling, though I didn't know why. I didn't want to talk, so I tugged on her shirt until she stopped. I said, "I'm going home. This place feels creepy."

All Karen did was make another noise that sounded even more like a chicken. I knew what it meant this time. It meant "chicken." She continued on.

I was afraid to go forward, but I guess I was more afraid to go back alone because I kept following. We walked through the tall weeds into a clearing, and it was soon apparent where the men had dug up the bone.

We stood by the edge of the hole, where I observed another large bone sticking out. From the look on her face, I knew Karen was also aware of it.

The bone was huge, and it was obvious that it was part of a ribcage, but I knew it wasn't even close to being big enough to be a mastodon's. But it definitely wasn't human, though it was the right shape. It was just too big.

We stood there, then I felt even more creepy. For some reason, I was beginning to feel that someone was watching us.

Suddenly, I heard a loud moan, like someone really large would make. I turned and ran like the wind. I didn't care if Karen thought I was a chicken—I would rather be a live chicken than a dead hero.

I ran as fast as I could, and I could hear Karen right behind me. I didn't stop at the old house but ran all the way back to the swimming hole, where I stopped only long enough to ease the burning in my side, then I ran again, all the way to my house. Karen was right on my heels.

We collapsed in my room, and I closed the window. I just couldn't get rid of that creepy feeling. I'd never felt anything like it, not even when I'd watched a forbidden R-rated horror movie Karen brought over while my parents were gone.

We just sat there, breathless, then finally, Karen said she was going home before it got dark. It was only about two in the afternoon, but I was kind of happy to have her leave, though I did feel scared about her walking home alone. I just wanted to forget the whole thing. I didn't understand it.

I couldn't sleep at all that night, and I imagined something big and dark walking around outside the house. I thought I was dreaming until I heard something bump into the siding, right where my bed was. I jumped up and went into my parents' bedroom and climbed into bed next to my mom.

She was surprised, as I hadn't slept with her since I was a toddler, but when she realized I was crying with fear, she let me stay. She kept telling me it was only a dream, but I knew better.

The next day, I went and spent the day at my Auntie Wilma's house while my parents were at work. No way I was hanging around home alone, and no way did I want to see Karen. I was afraid she would want to go back out to the old house. I was still scared to death, and I had no idea why, but my instincts were telling me something was wrong.

That night, I could once again hear something big circling the house. I snuck into my parents' room again, this time waking them up and whispering for them to listen.

They could hear it, and I know they were scared, too. My dad didn't have a gun or anything, and after a while, he called the police. By the time they got there, it was gone.

We were all awake by then, and my dad asked me what was going on, so I told him.

I told all about the house and the men with the bone and finding the rib cage and how big it was and everything. I told him about how something was watching us and how spooked I'd been and how I ran and ran and how the thing had bumped the wall where my bed was. I talked so fast I'm not sure they even caught it all.

My parents had no idea what to do, so we all just sat around and talked until we were too sleepy to talk any more, then we all just kind of fell asleep there in the living room. My dad was in the big easy chair and me and my mom were on the couch. The doors were locked and the curtains closed, so we felt pretty OK at that point, except I woke up with a sore neck.

I hadn't heard a peep from Karen, and then that next day, she called me. It was highly unusual for her not to come over all day every day.

"Something weird's going on, Cora. Something's been stalking all around our house at night and making weird sounds."

I told her we were having the same problem, and I knew it had something to do with the bones.

She paused for a long time. I was expecting her to argue with me as usual, but this time she didn't.

"What do you think it is?"

"Maybe a mastodon ghost."

I expected her to laugh, but she didn't.

"Like in that weird movie I brought over?"

"Yeah, except that was a human ghost, not a mastodon."

"Well, duh," she replied sarcastically. "We need an exorcist."

"Right. A mastodon exorcist."

"This isn't funny, pipsqueak."

"It was your idea to go over there, not mine," I replied.

"You always follow me around like a little puppy. You didn't have to go."

I could feel our friendship faltering. It had been on a shaky foundation for some time. What she was saying was true enough, but there was an element there that I had somehow mistaken for authority and leadership.

"Be careful out there, Karen," I said with an air of finality, knowing she planned to go back to the old house.

She was oblivious to what I was trying to tell her, or else she just didn't want to hear it.

"I'm going back. Are you going with me or are you going to stay home like a chicken?"

"Stay home like a chicken," I replied.

"I can conduct ambushes just fine on my own," she threatened.

"Fine by me," I answered, then hung up. I had never stood up to her before, but fear can motivate one in strange ways. There was no way I was ever going back out there, and I figured she wouldn't go without me.

That night, Karen called me back. She sounded truly terrified.

"Cora, I'm here alone. My mom's working tonight at the hospital and dad's out of town. Mom doesn't want me here alone. Can I come over? Please? I'm sorry about this afternoon."

My mom went and got her. When they arrived, Karen looked terrible. My mom made us some hot chocolate, and we went back into my room. I actually felt better with her there, as I wouldn't be alone.

We tried to watch something on TV, but neither of us was very interested, so we turned it off, got into our jammies and crawled into bed, turned out the lights, and talked. I could hear my mom and dad still up, talking about something in the living room, and it was comforting, even though it sounded a bit like an argument.

Karen started telling me about this thing that had terrorized her house and had both her and her mom scared to death, and how they'd called the police, who had come and found big footprints all over the yard. We talked and talked until it was late, then we both finally gave in to our sleep deprivation and went to sleep, curled up with the covers over our heads.

The night was quiet, with no strange noises.

That morning, while we were eating breakfast, my dad had the radio on listening to the news when the announcement came.

Two homeless men had been found dead out at the old Blane Place, and it appeared they'd been digging up the old pioneer graveyard out there. After the police investigation, the county had sent in a backhoe to push the dirt back onto the graves and cover everything back up.

There was no mention of the odd size of the bones, nor how the men were murdered, except the announcer had said that the deaths had occurred under mysterious circumstances and appeared to have possibly been from some kind of wild animal attack.

Karen and I just looked at each other, and if the thought of going back out there to check it all out crossed either of our minds, it didn't stay there long.

After that, Karen pretty much stopped coming over. I guess she found someone else to string along, or maybe it was because seeing me reminded her of how scared she had been. I don't know, but I soon had a boyfriend to hang out with, even though he was younger, only seven.

But we never had another visit from whatever had slammed the side of the house. We eventually moved away, and I lost track of Karen, but I bet, like me, she never forgot that day out in the Bigfoot graveyard.

The Sinkhole

Most of the stories I hear take place in the western U.S. I've often wondered if this is because there are more Bigfoot out West or if it's because the majority of my clients come from that part of the country. I do sometimes hear stories from other areas, and this is one that I found particularly interesting. I think you will, too. —Rusty

I was born and raised in the area of the Missouri Ozarks around Alley Springs. If you've ever visited there, you'll know that it's an area of karst limestone that erodes into sinkholes and caves. The woods there are thick and lush and beautiful, but it's not really a place very well-suited for two young boys to be out exploring, as it's very easy to get lost.

Well, me and my friend Jack were always out doing exactly that—exploring the thick deep woods of that part of the Ozarks. It's a wonder we never did get lost, but we seemed to both have a pretty good sense of direction.

We were boy scouts, and we'd learned to take care of ourselves through little tricks like telling direction from the arc of the sun, moss growing on the north side of trees, stuff like that.

But there was one day that really awakened us to the mysteries and possible dangers of our explorations, and after that day, we really slowed down a lot on going out wherever we wanted. We pretty much stuck to our well-known haunts after that.

We both had .22 rifles, which was very common for kids to have back then, because everyone hunted. I think we were both in our early teens when this happened. A lot of families in that area were what people call hillbillies, poor and uneducated, as well as pretty superstitious.

Not to put these people down, as they're my own folks, but that's just how it was. Of course, there was also a level of knowledge about the woods and natural remedies that people who didn't know that country didn't have, so it was a mixed bag of ignorance and high-level knowledge.

One reason everyone went hunting was because we were all pretty poor, and this was how a lot of families managed to keep food on the table—that and growing their own gardens and canning. We were way ahead of the survival movement, the living off-the-grid folks. My family didn't even have indoor plumbing when I was growing up.

The meat of choice was basically squirrel, as that was about all we could easily hunt. During season (and sometimes out of season), our dads would usually go get a deer or two, which was also one of our main staples. But we boys were encouraged to go squirrel hunting any time we wanted, and I intend to die without ever tasting squirrel meat again.

So, Jack and I took off one sunny day to go get a couple of squirrels for dinner. We were both pretty decent shots, and we really enjoyed the wandering in the woods part of the deal, though I was never crazy about killing anything.

I later inherited my dad's old rifle, but I haven't hunted in many years. Actually, thinking about this, I'm inclined to say that this incident pretty much took my interest in exploration and hunting away permanently, though we still went out some.

Jack and I were just walking along through the thick woods on a deer trail, real quiet, looking for squirrels, when all of a sudden he held up his hand for me to stop and listen, which I did.

We both stood there for a bit, and there was nothing, just the normal sounds of the forest, trees creaking, frogs, cicadas, that kind of thing.

Jack whispered to me, "I heard something coming from over that way." He pointed into the thick forest to our left.

"I didn't hear it," I replied. "What do you think it was?"

"Dunno. Maybe deer."

We stood there for a bit, listening—then from nowhere, it came through loud and clear. Neither of us had ever heard anything like it, at least not out in the Missouri woods. We strained to hear better, then looked at each other incredulously.

"It sounds like a baby crying," I whispered. "How in heck could a baby be way out here?"

"There must be people over there. Let's go this way and avoid them."

We turned to our right and stepped off the deer trail into the thick woods. We would bushwhack a bit until we got on another deer trail. There were deer and animal trails all over the place. One just had to be aware of what direction they were going so as not to get lost.

We both got our bearings, then continued on. But it wasn't long until we stopped, listening again. The crying baby was now ahead of us.

This was disconcerting. We didn't want to meet up with anyone out here, especially someone with a baby, because that would probably mean they were squatting out here and who knows, they might try to take our guns or something. There were some truly poor people around, and sometimes they were desperate.

We stopped, and after a while, continued on, this time veering back again to our left, through dense oak and hickory woods beneath massive bluffs. We were soon back on the deer trail we'd been following originally.

We trekked along, as quiet as we could, and after a while we sort of forgot about the people and once again focused on squirrels, but we saw nothing, which was very unusual. The woods were full of critters, and we would usually have bagged a couple of squirrels by that time and be on our way home.

Jack stopped again, holding up his hand.

"Did you notice anything weird?" he asked.

"Not really, except that crying baby."

"Well, just be still and listen for a minute."

We stood there, straining to hear, then I finally replied, "It's too dang quiet. There ain't a sound out here."

Jack nodded his head in agreement. "Yeah, it's weird. I'm thinking we should go home."

We had both been raised on stories of the supernatural, of ghosts and strange floating lights and ball electricity and other Ozark traditions, and neither of us was wanting to add any new stories to the hillbilly arsenal by having some weird adventure.

Little did we know that we would anyway, and our story would become an Alley Springs classic. In fact, I think it may be in some college's archives, as some professor was out there collecting stories not too long after all this happened. But that's another story.

OK, we decided to turn around and go home. But just then, and now behind us, we could hear that dang baby crying again. It was now starting to raise the hackles on my neck. How in heck could a baby cover that much territory that fast, even if someone was carrying it?

Shoots. We were both pretty freaked out now. We stood there for a bit in the shadows and thick brush, and soon the crying was closer. I kind of thought maybe I would start crying myself if it got any nearer. It then dawned on me how loud that baby was crying. It was unnatural.

We weren't sure what to do, so we veered off to our left. The crying somehow stayed behind us, keeping pace with us, so we went forward, abandoning our plans to go straight home. We'd have to circle around a bit to avoid this baby thing.

We went forward for a while, then Jack started veering back to our right. But just then, the baby crying came from that direction, so he headed left again. We were both starting to panic.

It felt like we were being herded or something, forced to go a certain direction. We talked about trying to circle around and get behind it to see what it was, but we couldn't go anywhere without it staying behind us.

Jack stopped, then whispered, "Monty, we're in trouble. We need a plan. These people are trying to push us in here and get us lost so they can ambush us. They must want our guns."

"We can hold them off with our rifles. We're armed, Jack, why be so scared? Let's just head home, and if we meet up with them, we'll shoot and scare them off."

"OK," he replied hesitantly, and we both turned around and started back the way we came. That put me in the front, and I sure as heck didn't want to be there. I wasn't sure if the rustling leaves I heard were from something in the woods or just from the breeze.

Now the baby crying was right smack in front of us. I stopped. I was totally scared to death at this point. Jack poked me in the back, but I stood firm. It felt like a trap, and no way was I going forward one more step.

We both just stood there, and then we could hear a rustling in the bushes, like someone coming our way. I stepped off the deer trail to the side and into the thick bushes, Jack right behind me.

The rustling stopped, then all of a sudden was over to our left again. I turned and went right, walking slow and silent, like Pappy taught me to do when we were close up on a deer. I was beginning to feel like I'd lost track of where we were, which was not a comfortable feeling. I'd been lost in these woods once as a young kid, and even though I'd managed to find my way home, it was something I'll never forget.

Oh boy. We both stood there, not sure what to do, but finally, Jack put his rifle to his shoulder and let go with a shot. The sound echoed through the woods. I think I jumped a good two feet in the air.

He then yelled out, "Y'all better leave us be now!"

"What'd you shoot at?" I whispered with concern.

"Nothing," he whispered back. "I just shot in the air, but I want them to know I mean business and not to mess with us."

But now things escalated, and we soon realized we weren't dealing with humans. We soon wished we were, even if they did mean us harm, because what we were dealing with turned out to be much more threatening.

From the thick forest behind us came a plaintive and mournful howl, thick as the woods with timbre and undulation. It was so loud my ears started to ring, making me want to cover them with my hands, but I refused to put my rifle down.

The look on Jack's face was a mirror image of the look on my own—a look of sheer terror. We were both frozen in place, but then, as if on cue, we both turned and ran the opposite way, away from the sound.

Suddenly, we were in a natural clearing, and we soon realized why the woods so suddenly ended. There was a small sinkhole ahead, one of many such sinkholes in that part of the Ozarks, where underground water dissolves the soluble limestone and dolomite and creates caves that sometimes collapse into sinkholes.

Jack was soon right next to me, huffing and puffing and looking red in the face and like he was about to cry. We both stood there, catching our breath, expecting the howler thing to come upon us and tear us apart, because we now knew it was something big from the sound it had made. It was unearthly.

But all was perfectly still. The thing seemed to have backed off. We collected ourselves, and when we both stopped puffing enough, that's when I heard it, a new sound, something coming from the sinkhole.

"Jack, there's something down in there," I said.

"I hear it," he replied. "It sounds like a dog whining."

"You go look and I'll cover you," I offered.

"Nah, it's our imaginations," he said.

We stood there some more, and I knew it had to be a dog.

"I'll go look and you cover me," I said.

"OK. Be careful," he replied.

I handed him my rifle, then got down on my hands and knees and crawled over to the edge of the sinkhole. Ozark sinkholes are often full of water because of the high water table, but this one was dry, to my surprise.

It was a pretty shallow one, maybe only eight feet deep, and sure enough, at the bottom sat a beagle. It looked just like one of my uncle's beagles he used for coon hunting.

I was shocked. What in hellsbells was a beagle doing out here? Had it followed a scent and fallen into the sinkhole? Surely a dog would have more sense than to just fall into a hole, I thought, but then, maybe it had come through at night. Had the thing that was making the moaning sound been chasing it?

I tried to reach down and grab it, but the hole was too deep. The poor thing looked bedraggled and scared to death and hungry. I loved my uncle's beagles and immediately felt a kinship with the little dog. We had to get it out somehow.

I crawled back over to Jack, then whispered, "There's a beagle in there. We have to get it out, but it's a good eight feet in."

I sat there at Jack's feet, thinking.

"You'll have to get in there and hand it up to me," he said.

"I'm too short," I responded. "You're the tall one, you get in there and hand it up to me, then I'll pull you out."

Jack didn't say a word, but he finally handed me the guns, then asked, "How are you gonna get me back out?"

"If worse comes to worse, I can throw in enough wood for you to stand on and gradually build it up so you can get out."

Jack didn't want to go in there, but he really was the taller of the two of us by a lot, and I knew he didn't want me to think he was a coward.

"What about that thing that was making the baby noise? What if it comes when you're getting me out?"

"I don't know," I said truthfully. "But we can't just leave that poor dog in there."

Jack was now on his hands and knees, crawling over to the edge of the sinkhole. Against my better judgement, I laid our rifles down and helped him slide down into the hole, where the little beagle looked up at us hopefully, wagging its tail. It looked kind of weak.

Jack was now beside it, petting its head and feeling its sides.

"He seems OK," Jack said. "I'm going to hand him up to you. Hook your heels on a bush so you don't get pulled in with us."

I did exactly that and reached down for the dog, which Jack had managed to pull up onto his shoulders. I was barely able to grab the dog by its collar, then I dragged it up, half choking the poor thing until I could grab its front paws.

"Don't let it get away," Jack said.

"How do I do that?" I asked, still hanging onto the dog's collar.

"Take off your belt and tie it to a tree."

I did as Jack said, the little dog licking me and weakly wagging its tail. It didn't look so good, like maybe it had been in there for a while.

That done, I then set to figuring out how to get Jack back out, all the while nervously eyeing the woods where we'd heard the loud howling. I had no idea what had made the sound, and I was hoping it had gone on its way and forgotten us.

I reached down for Jack, but I couldn't reach his hand. I then started looking around for a log or something to throw down to him. I found a couple of good sized rocks and managed to drag them over to the hole, then carefully roll them in, trying not to whack him on the head.

He stood on the rocks and this helped, but I still couldn't quite reach him. The little dog was now sitting there, tied to the bush, licking its paws. I needed to find a log, but there was nothing in immediate sight, and I was terrified to enter even the edge of the woods.

I finally forced myself to go into the forest, and sure enough, there, about 20 feet away, was a nice log that I knew would do the trick. I had to roll it back and forth a bit to release it from all the plants growing around it, but I finally freed it and started dragging it to the sinkhole.

It was heavy and wet and crumbly, and after a few feet, I stood up straight to catch my breath.

And that's when I saw it.

I nearly passed out from sheer terror and fear. There, standing not more than 10 feet from where I'd grabbed the log, was a huge creature, black as night and upright like a human, its head having a conical shape and its eyes big and liquid and unblinking.

Its legs were as big around as my uncle's water barrel, and its arms were thick and muscular and hung down beyond its knees just a bit. It had a look to it like a creature that was intelligent, and I say this because of the expression on its face and the look in its eyes.

My instincts said to run for my rifle, which was still where I'd left it when helping Jack into the sinkhole, but I was frozen in place. I just stood there, looking at it, and it looking back at me.

After what seemed like an eternity, it turned and walked away, and I remember being amazed at how quietly something that large could walk. I just stood there as it blended back into the forest and disappeared.

I was still terrified, and yet I somehow knew it wouldn't harm me. How I knew that, I don't know, and even though it had turned away and left, it could've easily returned, but I knew it wouldn't.

I was shaking, but I had the presence of mind to continue dragging the log over to the sinkhole, and I soon had it upturned and pushed down so it leaned against the side of the hole. Jack was able to shimmy part way up it and I grabbed onto him and pulled him the rest of the way. We left the log in the hole.

I collapsed next to the little dog.

"Let's get out of here," Jack said in a panic. "That thing has to still be around. Why are you just siting there?"

I told Jack what I'd seen. I know if he hadn't heard it howling, he wouldn't have believed me, but given that, he turned white as a sheet. He untied the beagle, picked up his rifle, and started back the way we'd come. I was right behind him.

We didn't hear any more babies crying or strange howls, and I thought several times we were lost, but we managed to finally get back home.

I was happy to be out of the woods. It was the last time I ever walked freely in them without wondering what might be watching me.

I took care of the beagle and it was soon OK, though it ate a bunch for a while. My folks put out the word, but we never found its owner. I named it Ricky, and we were friends for many years until he died of old age. He was a sweet little dog and a good companion, and I still miss him all these years later.

Jack and I still went squirrel hunting—we didn't have much choice in the matter, as it was part of our families' diet. I will say we both were very careful where we went, and we never went alone or unarmed. And though Jack didn't see the creature, I know he believed me. He never walked freely in the woods again either.

We had many conversations about that day, and we both decided that the Bigfoot was trying to herd us over to Ricky so we could save him. Why didn't the Bigfoot just save the dog itself? I don't know, as it was a pretty big creature and probably could've easily climbed into the hole and back out again. I just don't know the answer to that.

Maybe it wasn't trying to herd us to Ricky, but it sure seemed that way, and once we were there, it disappeared and left us alone.

In any case, I got a good dog friend out of the deal, even though the image of that creature will be seared into my mind forever.

The Tranquil Bigfoot

I met the fellow who told the following story out near Gardner, Montana. He was driving a government truck and saw me fishing the Yellowstone River and stopped to talk. I'll never forget the story he told, even though it took quite a bit of conversation before he felt comfortable enough with me to tell it.

It's a good one, and I must say he's not the first person I've met who believes Bigfoot wanders Yellowstone National Park, even though this incident took place not far out of the park boundary.

So be careful when you come up to one of those remote hot springs—you might just surprise one of the big guys having a good soak—Rusty

I'm a wildlife biologist. When people find this out, they always think I lead a life of outdoor adventure, which is actually rarely the case. I probably spend more time indoors in an office writing up reports and doing surveys than I do outdoors, especially in the winter.

But there was one time that I bet few can match for excitement, or maybe I should call it adventure—or maybe there are better words for that day, such as disbelief, wonder, and terror.

And believe me, none of my scientific colleagues know this story—well, with one exception—a fellow employee who is sworn to secrecy. I know she'll keep her pledge since she saw the same thing once.

It was early winter, and I was out in the forest trying to do a wolf count. This happened in the Yellowstone Park area, not far from the Lamar Valley, where packs of wolves tend to hang out. I worked for a state agency, not the park, but I can't say any more about that—it would be too easy to figure out who I am, as I still work there.

I carried a dart gun with tranquilizer darts because there was a lone wolf, a female, that I wanted to radio collar. Normally one would never do this kind of work alone, but there just wasn't anyone else available to go out with me. I really wanted to be able to collar this particular wolf if I happened to come across her, which was unlikely. But I wanted to be ready, just in case.

Winter is a good time to observe wildlife in the Yellowstone area as the grizzly bears are hibernating and not a problem. Otherwise, one has to be really cautious. But in winter, about all you have to worry about are the bison, and they aren't much of a worry, really, as they stick together and you can easily avoid the herds.

So, I was creeping along in the cover of the trees on the edge of a valley, stopping all the time to use my binoculars and scout around. A few times I saw movement down by the river, but it always turned out to be coyotes.

I came across a beautiful herd of bison in the distance, but nothing really unusual. It was a cold crisp day with sunny blue skies, perfect weather for what I was doing, and I was really enjoying myself. I really liked my job when I wasn't stuck indoors.

I slowly snowshoed along the small valley I was in, staying at the edge of the trees, stopping a lot to scope things out, looking for wolves. The snow was only a foot or so deep, so the going was easy. I felt like a mountain man, as I had the whole place to myself—well, me and the animals.

I carried a daypack with my lunch and a thermos of hot tea with lots of sugar for energy, and I finally decided it was time to sit down on a rock and enjoy a bite to eat. I was on a rise, and a breeze had picked up and was cooling things down, but it was still pretty nice if you sat in the direct sun. But even though it was only about one p.m., I knew I only had another couple of hours before I needed to head back, as the sun set by five and I was a good hour or so in.

I finished my sandwich and was sipping some hot tea from my thermos when I noticed what looked like a pair of wolves across the valley. I was excited, and quickly got out my binoculars.

Sure enough, it was a wolf pair, and I forgot all about my tea, watching them with a thrill. I had helped collar some of the wolves in the area and had subsequently developed a great interest in their well-being, but I didn't recognize this pair.

They were nonchalantly walking along the edge of the forest, heading for the river, probably on their way for a drink. Sure enough, they were soon at the water, drinking. As I watched, I suddenly heard a strange noise coming from the forest downhill from me, on my side of the river. It sounded like something big moaning in pain.

The wolves stopped in their tracks and looked up at where the noise was coming from, paused for a brief moment, then skedaddled back into the forest they'd come from, not wasting any time, loping along and kind of looking over their shoulders. They soon disappeared into the thick timber.

Well, this gave me pause, because there's not much that a wolf is afraid of. In fact, I'm not sure there's anything, except humans, and they didn't seem to be aware of me. Whatever had made that sound had scared them.

I sat there, wondering what was going on, when I heard it again. It was definitely an animal in distress, and it sounded like something big. I wondered what was going on, my instincts telling me it was time to go home.

I usually listen carefully to my instincts, especially after spending so much time in a wilderness that has plenty of apex predators, but for some reason my curiosity overran my fears. After all, I was a wildlife biologist, and I was wondering what kind of animal would make a sound like that. I knew all the bears were in hibernation. Was there a wounded bison over there? That's about all I could figure could make such a deep moaning sound. I had never heard anything like it.

I've seen wounded animals before, and I knew better than to get near them, but I guess my tranquilizer gun gave me a sort of false bravado. If there were a wounded animal nearby, my training said not to mess with it, to just let nature take its course, but my scientific curiosity got the better of me. I also carried a rifle—a 30.06—so if worse came to worse, I could shoot it and put it out of its misery. I hated to see anything suffer.

I decided that I would carefully skirt over there and see what it was, be extra cautious, then head back to my truck. It couldn't be all that far over to where the sound had come from, and it was on my side of the river. I put my pack back on and felt like I was prepared for whatever it was.

Well, I wasn't prepared at all, I found out.

As I quietly skirted the trees, the moaning sounded out again, and it was truly heart rending. It almost sounded human, and I stopped. What if it was a human? That would explain why the wolves had fled—in fact, that's about the only explanation I could come up with.

But a human could never make a sound that loud. It was a deep and distinct sound, something more like a bison or large animal would make, and it almost shook the ground I was standing on. I was puzzled, but again continued, walking very quietly and watching where I put my feet so as to not step on branches and alert it.

The creature moaned again and again, each time giving me pause and making me want to flee, but also showing me where it was, like a directional beacon. Because I was going so slow, it took me quite a while to get to it, but when I did, I felt like someone must feel who discovers a new species.

I had crept in behind some big rocks, and when I got the courage to peek around them, I was shocked beyond words.

There, lying on the ground on its side as if it were too weak to fight anymore, was a man-like being about the size of a human teenager, but covered from head to toe in slick reddish-brown hair. Its back was to me, but I could see it had something wrong with it. It was partially hidden behind some shrubs so that I couldn't quite make out what was going on.

Now the creature raised itself on its elbows and moaned again, the immensity of the sound taking my breath away. Whatever it was, it had one good pair of lungs. The sound was way louder than one would expect from something that size.

It now tried to scoot itself along on its hips, then stopped, obviously in pain and somehow weighed down. Did it have a broken leg or something? If so, I would be obligated to shoot it. But how could I shoot something that seemed so human?

I was pondering what to do more than trying to figure out what it was, which I did later—in fact, I became obsessed with trying to classify it. I tried to get a better vantage point, but I just couldn't see what was the matter.

I stood there, hidden, for some time, not sure what to do. I was thinking it was a monkey or gorilla of some kind, but I had no idea why it would be in the wilds near Yellowstone. Maybe it had escaped some private zoo. You know how your mind tries to make sense of something it can't figure out, something so foreign that it makes no sense to you, so you just keep mulling it over and over.

I knew I had to do something and couldn't just stand there any longer, so I inched my way around to where I could see better. I was still behind it, but I could now see that its foot was caught in some kind of trap. It looked to be an old bear trap of some kind and looked all rusted out.

The creature would try to pull off the trap with its big hands, then moan from the pain, unsuccessful. I had no idea how long it had been there, but there was blood on its foot and all around on the snow, so I knew it had been trapped for some time, bleeding. I felt sick thinking of the pain it must be in, as the huge jaws of the trap looked pretty well entrenched in the flesh of its foot.

I knew there was no way I could help it without getting up close to it to spring the trap. I'd come across animals in traps before, but never in the park, as it was totally illegal to trap there. I'd always had someone with me to help, and we would generally either tranquilize and release it or shoot the animal if there was nothing we could do.

I got out my tranquilizer gun. I would just have to tranquilize it and release it and let it go on its way to recovery or death, but that was all I could do.

I put my gun to my shoulder and shot a dart into its back between the shoulder blades where it couldn't reach it. The animal jumped, startled. I knew the darts had to sting a bit, but not too bad. It turned towards me, but couldn't move enough to look my way.

After a while, I knew I needed a second dart, so I reloaded and shot it again, then waited some more, trying to quit shaking. Now the animal was nodding its head down onto its chest, and I knew it was time to move in. I had no idea how long the effect would last on something this big, as the largest animal I'd ever tranquilized was a wolf.

I very cautiously moved closer, picking up a long stick, then poking it a bit to see if it would react. It didn't, so I quickly went to the trap and was able to spring it, though it was difficult. The trap was old and rusted, and I guess it had been set many years ago. The poor creature had unwarily stepped into it.

I pulled the big teeth of the trap away from the creature's flesh, which wasn't easy, as it had dug deep. I didn't want to contribute to the damage, but I had to get it off.

The foot was a mess, and I felt really bad for the animal. I had no idea if it could survive this, and even if it did, if it would be able to walk again and forage or hunt for food and water. I was again tempted to just shoot it and put it out of its misery, but it just seemed wrong. Keep in mind that I hadn't seen its face at this point, as I was too busy springing the trap.

I got up and went back to where I'd left my pack by the rocks, getting out my first-aid kit. It had only a few essentials in it, but one of those was a small bottle of iodine. All government field employees in my region had to take first-aid courses, so I had an idea of what to do.

I tried to clean out the wound a bit and then poured the whole bottle onto it, hoping it would help keep it from getting infected. I wondered if I should wrap it, but I decided the creature would just take it all off.

Now I had to get out of there, as there was no more I could do, and who knew how long I had before the animal woke up. As I stood to go, I saw it move a bit. Its head had been resting on its left cheek, turned away from me, but now I saw it had turned its head back and its eyes were open, watching me.

I could now see its face, and I was stunned. It looked exactly like a human, but with a larger brow and a flat nose, and of course, it was much bigger. Its eyes were glazed with the sedative, but I knew it was awake enough to know what was going on. It watched me intently, and I immediately stepped back, then turned and ran like hell in sheer shock and fear as I realized what I was seeing.

I had never seen anything like it, and I hoped I never would again. All I know is I picked up my gear and ran as fast as my legs would carry me on snowshoes until I had to slow down because my lungs were burning in pain. I was too scared to even look back, but I could imagine it at my heels, which in retrospect was unlikely, given its condition.

It was almost dark when I got back to my truck, threw my pack onto the front seat, and jumped in, looking over my shoulder the whole time. I drove as fast as prudent back down the long and rough slick road.

I took the next week off, saying I was ill. I couldn't sleep at night, and I kept thinking something was trying to break into my house. I would dream strange shadowy dreams of manlike beasts trying to get me, large dark monsters limping through my back pasture and coming to the house and trying to break in.

Finally, after a week, my mind started calming down a bit, even though I was still in somewhat of a state of shock. I returned to work, but I told my boss I couldn't do any more wolf counts for a while as I was still too sick.

I ended up taking several months of leave without pay and spending time with my cousin at his place in Bozeman, Montana, recovering my balance. I had no idea such a creature existed, and I was too embarrassed to even talk about it to anyone, as I didn't want people to think I was going insane.

Finally, I returned to work, and months later, I was taking a coffee break with a fellow employee who had been out in the field the previous week doing the wolf work I had been assigned but couldn't do.

She informed me she was going to ask for a transfer because she wanted to go to some place warmer. This really shocked me, as I had thought working with wolves was one of her life dreams. I suspected something had happened.

I flat out asked if she'd seen something unusual. She looked at me kind of funny, but refused to talk about it. I decided to tell her about my experience, and she listened intently.

Finally, she started sobbing and shaking. I tried to reassure her, and it was then that she told me what she'd seen, not more than a month after I'd seen it.

Not far from where I'd taken off the trap, over on the other side of the valley, she'd been sitting in the trees watching for wolves and had instead seen a dark creature walk on two legs down to the river where it bent down and drank. It then stood, looked directly her way, and started towards her.

She had panicked and was ready to run when it turned and walked the other way. She quickly retreated, running to her truck, just as I had done, scared to death.

We talked about it for a while, both agreeing it had to be a Bigfoot. And sure enough, it had a limp, but seemed otherwise fine.

I have no idea if it realized I'd saved its life and was thereby disposed favorably towards humans, or if it also realized that a human had made the trap that almost cost it its life. I'll never know, but my co-worker decided to stay, though neither of us will work in that area without someone else with us.

We later found out that one of Yellowstone's most prominent backcountry rangers had seen these beasts numerous times in the park and firmly believed in them, going on the record after he'd quit his job.

So I guess we're not nuts after all.

The Imaginary Friend

I don't hear too many Bigfoot stories from the state of Wisconsin, though I don't doubt they're there. I've often wondered why people expect Bigfoot to be found only in the Pacific Northwest and Canada, as I'm sure they can migrate to any place that has suitable habitat, as do most animals, including humans.

This story was told on a flyfishing trip with a group on the Yampa River in Colorado at one of my favorite fishing holes. — Rusty

When we were kids, my little brother, Tim, had an imaginary friend—well, at least we all thought his friend was imaginary, until we found out he wasn't.

This happened when Tim was five and I was eight. We lived on a dairy farm in rural Wisconsin. I was old enough to help with the chores, but since Tim was so young, he got to do what he wanted, which was mostly to hang around and watch me and our older brother, Matt, take care of the cows.

But Timmy would get bored and go do his own thing after a while. That's when he was supposedly hanging out with his imaginary friend back in the trees that bordered the big cow pasture. There was a small stream there, and I had taught him to fish in it, though I don't think it had any fish, as I'd never seen any.

Now, in case you think we were all remiss by letting a five-year old hang out by himself by a stream in the deep woods, let me add that the stream was so small Tim could easily wade it without hardly getting his ankles wet, and if you walked through the trees for about 30 feet, you were on the neighbor's farm, also a dairy. There just wasn't much Tim could do to get himself into trouble—or so we all thought.

So, after he'd help throw hay to the cows and then watch us milk, Tim would always disappear into the trees, where he'd sit on a rock and "go fishin'," which meant just sitting there with a string in the water.

Timmy was a happy little guy, easy going, a trait he still has and that makes him really popular. He now owns an art gallery in Jackson, Wyoming, which I never would've predicted of a Wisconsin farm boy.

He's good with people and has friends from all over the world. He's always smiling and happy. I think this is what drew his imaginary friend to him, that and maybe also his age.

Well, it was mid-summer when Timmy came home from fishing one morning and announced that he had this new friend. Nobody paid much attention except me, and I asked who his friend was and where he'd met him.

I knew it couldn't be real, as the neighboring farmers were ready to retire and their kids were long gone—they were the only people Tim could possibly visit with, as nobody else lived nearby. The rest of the countryside was our own hay fields and cow pastures.

"Who's your new little friend, Timmy?" I asked.

"He's not little, he's big. He's an old man," Tim replied.

"Oh? An old man? Where'd you meet him?"

"He lives by the Big River." This is what Tim called the little stream, which was more of a brook, actually.

"How'd you meet him?"

"He came over to where I was fishin' and gave me a present. See?"

Tim held out a shiny rock. It looked like all the other rocks around.

"Nice, Timmy. What's his name?"

"I don't know. He can't talk like we do."

"Can't talk? Why not?"

"His lips are too big. He just makes funny noises."

"What kind of funny noises?"

Tim stood up and started jumping around, making noises like a monkey. I laughed. That's when I knew he was making it all up.

"Well, bring him to the house for dinner sometime. Mom and Dad would like to meet him, I bet."

Tim looked at me like I was crazy.

"No they wouldn't," he replied, then headed off to his room.

I told my parents about what he'd said, and they laughed and commented on his overactive imagination. None of us gave it another thought, and all summer Tim would come home and tell us about his friend, who he'd now dubbed

"Sampson" after some guy in a Bible story Mom had read to him. Timmy said his friend had long hair and was strong, like Sampson.

"Sampson sits in the stream and I pour water over his head when it's hot," Tim said one day. "He's covered with hair and is taller than I am even when he's sitting down."

"Wow, he must be one big dude," Matt replied.

"What do you use to pour water over him?" I asked.

"An old pitcher I found."

"Where'd you find it?"

"In the old cupboard in the living room."

"Timmy," Matt said patiently, "That's grandma's old lemonade pitcher. It's an antique. If Mom finds out you have it out there, she's gonna be real mad."

"What's an antique?" Tim asked.

"Something old," I replied.

"Sampson's an antique," Tim said.

"What does he eat out there?" Matt asked.

"I don't know," Tim answered, then took off for the stream.

That was the start of Tim wanting food to take out to his friend. After that, he would always ask for an extra cookie or apple or whatever was around to take out. Mom thought it was cute that he was being so considerate, even if it was all imaginary, and would give him whatever he wanted, figuring he was just eating it himself.

Tim was now spending most of his time down by the stream. We rarely saw him any more, except for lunch and at the end of the day. Mom started worrying about him a bit. I heard her and Dad and Matt talking about it one evening. They wanted to make him stay home more but weren't sure how to do that without him thinking he was being punished.

Tim was always bringing home "gifts" from his imaginary friend—rocks, twigs, and things one finds outdoors. He would always talk about how Sampson gave him the gifts in exchange for a cookie or an apple or some such thing, and he would keep the gifts on a shelf in his bedroom.

But one day, Tim came back from the stream with a dead bird. It was small, a sparrow, and he carried it very gingerly and looked like he might cry.

"Sampson gave me this bird for a present, but it's dead," Tim said sadly.

I figured Timmy had found the dead bird.

"Why would he give you a dead bird?" I asked.

"I don't know. Maybe he thinks I can help it."

"Maybe he killed it," Matt said. Tim gave him a look of surprise and shock.

"Sampson would never kill nuthin'," Tim replied testily.

Timmy took the bird on up to the house, and Mom didn't take too kindly to seeing it.

"Tim, dead birds can have lice and parasites on them. Next time you find one, you just leave it be," she scolded him.

"But Sampson gave it to me," Tim protested.

Dad had now come up from the barn. "I think this Sampson thing is getting out of hand," he said. "Tim, I'm going to start finding things for you to do around the farm. You can start helping us with cleaning up, OK?"

Tim looked pleased. He'd always been told he was too little to help out, but now he was going to be included with the big guys—me and Matt.

I slapped him gently on the shoulder.

"You're going to be milking before you know it," I said.

But now Tim looked upset. "Does this mean I can't go see Sampson?"

Dad answered, "No, Timmy, you'll still have time to go see your friend. But we need your help, and now that you're almost six, it's time to start learning the ways of the dairy."

Matt and I hadn't really started doing much in the way of chores until we were about seven, but I knew my parents wanted Tim to stay closer to home, so they were going to find things for him to do.

So, all of a sudden Tim was busy all day helping around the farm. Dad found him chores that really didn't need doing, things like raking up the straw that had been kicked out of the cow barn, which would normally have just been left and gradually blown away or been stomped into the ground. Dad didn't want to work Timmy too hard, so he gave him chores that were easy but that would keep him busy.

Tim was now pleased to be a part of the farm, like one of the hands, but he also chafed somewhat at not being able to go hang out at the stream with his imaginary friend.

After a week or so of doing chores, he began to just disappear in the middle of doing things, then would come back and resume his task after an hour or so. Dad got after him, but this only led to Timmy taking off when Dad was too busy to notice.

It was now almost the end of summer, and when school started, there wouldn't be a problem, because Tim wouldn't have time to go down to the stream. He'd be in kindergarten all afternoon.

Autumn was in the air. The leaves were starting to turn yellow, and the grasses were now dried and gone to seed.

One day, Mom came out to the barn where I was cleaning the milking equipment and said she'd heard a weird noise and told me and Matt to go find Timmy. She was worried.

She described the sound as a deep bellowing, kind of like a bull or something, but it was off in the distance, on up the stream a ways. Tim had been helping her shell some sweet peas, but had disappeared when she'd gone inside to answer the phone.

Matt and I looked at each other, then took off as fast as we could go. But before we could get down to the stream, here came Timmy, running as fast as he could. We were glad to see him, but wondered why he was running.

He came up to us and stopped, gasping for air.

"Hurry! There's a fire coming down the stream! We have to get the cows out of the barn!"

The cow barn was in the trees next to the stream, which were now bending from a stiff breeze that was picking up, probably ahead of an early fall storm.

"It's OK, Timmy, it's OK," I said, looking all along the trees for smoke. "I don't see any smoke. How do you know there's a fire?"

Tim was still puffing, but he managed to say, "Sampson told me there's a fire coming. Hurry! We have to get the cows out!"

Matt shot me a knowing look. Tim pretending he had a friend was one thing, but this was going a bit beyond the pale. Dad would not be happy if we ran the cows back out of the barn. They always found their way into the barn from the big pasture at milking time, and to run them back out would upset them and make them hard to catch and milk.

"Timmy, I thought you said Sampson can't talk," I said. "How could he tell you there was a fire?"

Tim was about to cry from frustration. He said, "Sampson pointed at the sun, then made a sound like fire and acted like it was burning him, then pointed back at the trees up the way. I know there's a fire coming, we have to get the cows out."

Now Tim took off running, me and Matt close behind. He was going to open the barn door himself and run the cows out. There would be hell to pay with Dad.

Matt looked as perplexed as I felt. What had come over Timmy? Why was he hell bent on getting the cows out? He would get in a lot of trouble, and surely he knew it. All I could figure was that he really thought there was a fire coming.

Just then, I turned and saw it—smoke! It was heavy, and coming down the creek fast, drifting through the thick timber. The leaves and understory were all dried out, and now I could see the fire, only a short distance away and coming faster than I could imagine. I yelled and pointed. Matt saw it and looked surprised. We both lit out for the barn.

By the time we got to the barn door, the fire had already roared down the creek like a tornado and was nearly on us. The door was open, and we jumped back as cows came spilling out, little Timmy chasing them from inside, yelling and twirling his jacket at them.

Matt ran them on into the pasture, while I made sure they were all out, yelling for Tim to go up to the house. I then ran outside and turned on the hose we used to fill the stock tanks and began spraying the side of the barn nearest the fire.

Dad was soon there, and he and Matt managed to drive the tractors away from the barn while I kept watering everything down. The fire was raging through the trees, and it was then that I heard a strange and unsettling scream, rising over the roar of the fire. It was the most eerie thing I've ever heard, and it came from right behind the barn, not far from the burning trees.

It scared me so bad that I dropped the hose and ran up to the house. I was soon inside, then me and Mom and Timmy came out and watched nervously from the big porch.

The house was up on a small rise, and we could see a good ways along the stream. It looked for a while like the barn might catch fire, as some of the elms right next to it were burning like hot torches, but the fire soon moved on down the creek, catching the tops of nearby trees like a firestorm.

The fire had finally moved on, leaving smoldering branches and burned understory behind, but fortunately the barn hadn't burned. I knew that my spraying it had saved it, and I also knew I wouldn't have done that if Timmy hadn't alerted us to the fire.

Man oh man, what a strange thing, having him come running up like that before anyone could even know there was a fire coming. Matt and I had stood there, looking for smoke or any indications of a fire in the distance and seen nothing. How had Tim known?

He maintained that his friend Sampson had told him, and he even held steadfast to this story when Mom and Dad questioned him. None of us knew what to think about it all.

One evening, not too long after, we were all sitting on the porch talking about it when a strange throaty shout reverberated from the trees along the stream. We couldn't see what had made it, even though most of the foliage had been burned.

Timmy stood and yelled back, "Goodbye, Sampson! See you next spring!"

To our surprise, the shout came back. It was deep and very loud and we all knew it could have only been made by a very creature.

We all set there in silence, trying to take in the idea that maybe Tim's friend had been real. The thought gave me chills.

"Where's he going, Timmy?" I asked.

"I don't know, but I think he goes where it's warmer for the winter. He tried to tell me something last night, but I couldn't really understand him."

"You were down there again last night?" Mom asked in horror. "Didn't we tell you not to go down there again? Especially with the fire—things are still smoldering and it's dangerous."

"It's OK, I don't want to go down there any more with Sampson gone," Tim answered.

"Well, I guess we should thank him for saving the barn and cows," Matt said.

"Too late," Tim answered. "Besides, I know you all thought he was just in my head."

We all sat there, looking at each other, none of us feeling very much like talking. With that, Tim got up and went inside and upstairs to his room. I followed him.

"Tim, I'm sorry I didn't believe you," I said contritely.

"It's OK," he answered with a grin. "Wanna see a sketch I made of Sampson?"

"Sure," I replied, though I wasn't sure I really did.

Tim handed me a drawing, and I just sat there, looking at it. Finally, I said, "Timmy, do me a favor and don't ever show this to Mom and Dad, OK? They would have a heart attack. Is this what you really saw all summer?"

"Yup," Tim answered. "That's Sampson."

I sighed and handed Tim the drawing of the huge black Bigfoot. And as far as I know, Tim never did show it to our parents. Sampson never came back, which I consider a good thing, in spite of his saving the cows and the barn from the fire.

Well, we all grew up and went on to other things, and like I said, Tim opened his gallery. The last time I went to visit Tim in Jackson, I asked him about Sampson, and he just laughed.

"I still have that sketch," he said.

"Was it real?" I asked.

"It was," he said. "As real as you and I, and I would give anything to see Sampson again, although now that I've lost my childhood innocence, I would probably have a heart attack."

We both grinned and toasted Sampson with a beer.

Come and Get Me

I find this story to be one of the more mysterious that I've heard, primarily because it involves the possibility of a Bigfoot following someone from one place to another more distant place hundreds of miles away—or was the first one just a dream or hallucination?

I met Kelly at a bookstore in Pocatello, Idaho, on my way back home to Colorado from fishing in Montana. She had just purchased one of my books to help get her students interested in reading. I really enjoyed hearing her story over a cup of coffee, and I must say she's one of the braver people I've ever met. — Rusty

My name is Kelly, and this happened a few years ago. It all started when I was waitressing at a truck stop in Boise, Idaho. It went on for some time, then ended abruptly, as you'll see.

I won't name the truck stop, as I prefer to stay anonymous and someone might figure out who I am. I say that because it was a really popular place, and I met a lot of people going through there.

It was actually a total zoo, but it had two things going for it: I was so darn busy that it kept me in good shape, and I made good tips. A lot of truckers are good-hearted guys, and when they saw how hard I worked, they'd leave a good tip. I managed to squirrel a lot of it away, which helped me later.

Well, to make a long story short, I was one busy gal because when I wasn't working, I had managed to get myself involved with a man who was a real nutcase and who kept me hoppin'.

He was about as needy as they come, and I guess it appealed to the mom in me at first, but I soon got tired of it. He just about wore me out. He couldn't stand to be alone, and he wanted me to wait on him hand and foot—I guess that's why he picked a waitress to date.

But I got tired of it and soon broke up with him. I was relieved, but I also found myself with lots of free time, which I wasn't used to having. I'm not much of a TV watcher, so I didn't know what to do with myself. It was then that I discovered the internet.

I had a little laptop that had been given to me by a friend on his way to jail for yet another DUI. He was an alcoholic, and it was his third offense. He knew he'd be in there for a while, so he gave me a bunch of his stuff.

I hadn't paid much attention to the computer, as I had no idea how to run it, but after I broke up with my boyfriend, I decided I should try to learn something new and maybe advance myself somehow. I didn't want to be a waitress for the rest of my life. It was too hard of work.

I figured it all out by myself, and the apartment I lived in had someone nearby who had a Wifi signal I could access. They hadn't put a password on it, so I was able to use their internet signal for free. Sometimes it got a little slow, but at least it was free. I'm pretty sure it belonged to the guy in the apartment above me, and he was always irritating me by making lots of noise all night, so I didn't feel a bit bad about using his internet.

At first, I just did the usual stuff, like read the news and a few blogs I'd discovered. But then I decided to check out some of the nearby towns to see if there were any jobs, as I was about fed up with Boise and wanted to leave.

So, I did a search on the name of a little town out in west Idaho, and I'll be darned if it didn't take me to this Bigfoot website that had lots of information, including a sighting near that town. I'd heard of Bigfoot, but I'd never paid it any mind, as I didn't believe for one minute it was possible to have a giant hairy ape in the woods and never have anyone find a dead body.

I read about the sighting, then I went and read all the sightings listed for Idaho, then I read about the neighboring states. Before long, it was time to go to work and I hadn't had a wink of sleep. I couldn't wait to get home that night to read more. For some reason, even though I didn't believe in it, I was suddenly all obsessed with Bigfoot.

I knew it was a way for me to forget my ex and also to escape from reality, which wasn't being so kind to me, as my car had broken down and I didn't want to spend the money to fix it. It was an old junker and not really worth it. So I would just sit and read Bigfoot stories and forget everything else. It was great entertainment.

I just let my old car sit there, and I started bumming a ride with a friend to work. When I wasn't working, I'd be on the internet reading about Bigfoot. This went on for months, and you would think I would've run out of stuff to read, but there's a lot on there—you'd be amazed, and more was added every day.

The only time I wasn't reading about Bigfoot was when I was working or doing things I had to do, like getting groceries or doing laundry or sleeping. Heck, part of the time I'd get so involved I would forget to go to bed until the middle of the night.

Then I discovered the Bigfoot forums. They fascinated me with all the different Bigfoot discussions, and a lot of the members said they'd seen a Bigfoot. I'd had no idea this was such a big thing.

Well after several months of this, I couldn't have told you if I'd ever even had a boyfriend, and I also forgot all about my car, which was eventually towed. I wasn't sure what attracted me to the topic of Bigfoot, but maybe it was the combination of mystery and adventure. I got to be pretty well-known on the forums, and I started to really want to make this my life's mission, to see a Bigfoot.

OK, this all sounds like fun and games, but at about that same time, I started getting paranoid that there really was a Bigfoot around. I lived in a big apartment complex, the last place a Bigfoot would hang out, and yet I got to where I was afraid to go outside at night. The building set on the edge of a big field that was spooky at night.

It was about then that I swore I saw a big head outside my window. It was late at night, and I lived on the second floor, so I never worried one bit about peeping Toms, but I felt like I was being watched. I jerked my head around real fast and there it was, a big shadow in the window. It was gone in a flash, but it scared me to death.

After that, I hung sheets over all the windows. How in hellsbells could something look through a second-story window? It would have to be really tall or else climb up onto my little deck.

As time went on, I got more and more scared. This progressed to where I would turn off the lights when I was home at night, then pull up the edge of one of the sheets and carefully look outside. I always thought I could see something big in the shadows, and I knew it was waiting for me.

After awhile, I decided I had to stop reading about Bigfoot. It was freaking me out too much. So, I went and got some books on crafts stuff, like how to make candles, and decided I'd start a little home business in my spare time. This would keep me busy and also maybe make me some extra money—much better than wasting time thinking about something that probably didn't even exist. I decided it was all my imagination.

I made scented candles and started selling them around town at some of the shops, and after a couple of months, they started selling pretty good. I was surprised, and I saved every extra penny I made. I wanted to buy another car, as I was getting tired of bumming off my friend, even though I would help buy her gas.

I finally got enough to buy a car, and I ended up with a small used Subaru station wagon. It had enough room in it that I could go for a trip and carry along camping gear or whatever I might need. I'd been wanting to take a vacation for a long time, and now I had a ride so I could go somewhere.

I was pretty excited, and I got on the internet to check out cool places I could go. I hadn't been on the internet much at all for some time, and of course, being me, I soon had to go check out some of the Bigfoot sites, even though I'd sworn off them.

My obsession was still there, even though I'd ignored it for some time. I read all the latest sightings, especially in Idaho, and when I was done, I didn't want to go anywhere. I was too scared to camp out, especially alone.

That night I went to bed and had nightmares, really bad ones, and they all had Bigfoot in them. I woke up in the middle of the night terrified. I was so groggy I just wanted to go back to sleep, but I forced myself to get up and walk around. I knew I couldn't go back to sleep, as I would have more bad dreams.

But then, there in my apartment in the middle of night, I started smelling something funny. I had read tons about Bigfoot, and I knew they sometimes had a bad odor, and I wondered if my dreams hadn't somehow been triggered by a real Bigfoot outside. I was getting ready to call my friend and ask her to come over when I realized what I was smelling was gas!

I got dressed, then grabbed my purse and car keys and fled outside, jumping into my car. I dialed 911 as I drove away. The further I got from my apartment, the more awake I felt, with the grogginess finally going away, leaving me with a headache.

I drove to the diner, where I had breakfast and coffee. I was so happy I had a car, otherwise who knows what would've happened, as they evacuated my apartment building and I would've had no way to go anywhere.

The gas leak was a big deal, with the building being evacuated for several days, and I went and stayed with my friend. When they finally let everyone come back after a few days, I went and got the few things I wanted to keep, loaded my car, and drove away. It was evening, and I swore I saw a big dark shadow watching me from the bushes nearby, and it gave me chills, but I just figured it was my imagination.

I called the diner and quit, just like that. I then went to my bank and cleaned out my account, getting it all in cash. I had enough money to live on for some time, and nothing was holding me back. I could go wherever I wanted.

I had no idea where to go, but I knew I wanted to go where there couldn't possibly be any Bigfoot. I was so spooked by all this that I just wanted to go live in the middle of a town where there were no woods for Bigfoot to hide in.

I guess that by then I was pretty much a confirmed believer, a long ways from the skeptic I'd been when I started reading about Bigfoot. In a lot of ways I really wished I'd never discovered the topic.

OK, so where to go? I didn't know whether to go east or west on the freeway, so I flipped a coin and ended up going west. I'd never been so free in my life, and it actually felt kind of uncomfortable.

After I'd been on the road for about an hour, I realized that I was going in the direction of my grandparents' house, which was a few hours away from Boise. My grandparents had died years ago, but I had fond memories of visiting them in their little town of Pocatello.

When I got there, which set in a pretty valley, I was shocked. The town was way bigger than I remembered it. I drove around, noting that the university there was really cool, like a world all to itself.

It suddenly dawned on me that I wanted to go back to school and make something of myself. I was sick of waitressing, and I knew I could do whatever I wanted, as I'd had good grades in high school. All of a sudden, I felt a sense of elation, like I finally had a real purpose in life.

I got a room in a cheap motel and stayed there until I found a nice little house to rent, right in a cozy neighborhood near the university. I bought some second-hand furniture and was soon settled in.

I remember standing on the front porch of that little house and being all happy because it all felt so secure and homey. I loved my new house and town, and I never wanted to leave. Bigfoot seemed far far away.

I enrolled in Idaho State University that fall, after finding work in yet another diner. I was sick of diners, but now I had a goal. I wanted to be a teacher.

I loved school, and I met some really nice people. All went well until one evening when for no apparent reason I started feeling really weird. I'd been studying, and I thought maybe I was getting sick.

That night, I had the same nightmares I'd had before, when I'd been in Boise. I'd decided that those been from the gas leak that had made me sick, but now here they were again.

I woke up around 2 a.m. All the dreams once again had Bigfoot in them, and I was really groggy, just like before. I managed to drag myself out of bed, afraid to go back to sleep, thinking I wouldn't ever wake up. This time, I had a weird and very vivid sensation like an icy wind flowing through my body. I was trembling and shaking.

I wandered around the house, but I didn't smell anything this time. I decide to step outside onto the little porch to clear my head. It was a nice warm night, really balmy, and the stars were hanging in the night sky like jewels.

As I set there, my mind began to clear, and I started feeling better. Why was I having Bigfoot nightmares? I hadn't read anything about Bigfoot for a long time, nor even thought about it.

Then, sitting there in an old wicker chair on my porch, I thought I saw movement over in the neighbor's yard. I figured it was probably a skunk or something, so I was suddenly on alert. Last thing I wanted was to tangle with a skunk in the middle of the night.

Sure enough, a skunky smell drifted over my way, so I decided to go inside. But as I turned to go, all of a sudden I felt a panic. I bolted through the door and locked it behind me. I stood there, leaning against the door, my heart racing and my hands all clammy.

I had no idea why I was so terrified, and I finally decided it must be the nightmares affecting me. I forced myself to calm down, then went into the kitchen and started the teapot. I would have a nice cup of peppermint tea before going back to bed. That would help calm me and settle me down.

As I sat there at the kitchen table in my robe, sipping hot tea with honey, I suddenly felt like I was being watched. But all the curtains were closed, and it was impossible for someone to see in.

It was then that I noticed the curtain on the back door that led into the kitchen was pulled aside just a few inches, and I swore I could see something shining, something like a flashlight—and it was red.

I soon realized I was looking straight into the eye of something that was standing there peeking in through the window, something taller than I was. I screamed and spilled my tea as I jumped up and fled into the living room.

I was now shaking as I dialed 911 on my cell phone. I got dressed and waited. It didn't take long for the police to arrive, and they looked all over, but didn't find anything.

After they left, I was still scared to death, but I managed to work up the courage to run to my car, which was parked right by the front door. I drove to the diner where I worked. I sat there the rest of the night drinking coffee, and finally went to my classes.

I was a wreck. I didn't know what to do and couldn't concentrate on my classes at all. I hardy even remember being there. After being up most of the night, I should've been totally half asleep, but I was totally buzzed on caffeine, I'd drank so much, and it made me really jittery.

I went home after class and tried to pull myself together. I had to have been hallucinating the whole thing, sort of a waking dream. My little house now felt cold and ominous, not at all like the refuge it had been earlier. I needed help.

I looked through the campus directory and called the health center, making an appointment with a counselor. I'd never gone to a counselor, but maybe they could help me. They had an opening that same day, which was fortunate for me, as I didn't think I could go through another night like that.

I went in with some trepidation. Would they think I was crazy? Maybe I actually was. If so, what could they do to help me?

OK, I came out afterwards with mixed feelings about counselors. Even though the woman who had seen me was very kind, she obviously thought I was nuts. She wanted me to come back for a bunch of tests to confirm it. She started talking about a possible personality disorder, and for some reason, this just didn't set well with me.

I mean, I'm usually pretty easy going, and none of my friends seemed to think I had anything wrong—in fact, they all said I was pretty pragmatic. Plus I never drank or did drugs, so that couldn't be the cause of my weird dreams—if they were just dreams.

OK, so now what? I really didn't want to spend another night there in my little cottage alone, but I didn't have the money to just go get a motel or something. I had a little tent and thought about going camping, but that just seemed like going straight into the fire—sure, go camp in the woods when you're scared of Bigfoot, that really makes sense.

So, I stayed home, scared to death, but determined I would conquer this thing, whether it was real or in my own head. At that point, I was seriously wishing I'd never heard of Bigfoot, yet alone done so much research on it. I wanted my innocence back, my carefree life before I'd discovered all this. But there was no going back, as they say. Another saying that came to mind was that the only way out is through.

I drank some peppermint tea to make me sleepy, then went to bed. Before I knew it, it was morning and all was well—no Bigfoot dreams.

I was pretty happy about that. Maybe it was all in my head and talking about it with the counselor had brought it to my consciousness more and helped solve it—or something like that. I sure wasn't much for psychology and knew almost nothing about it.

That evening, when I came home, I got on the internet and started checking out sleep disorders. A friend at school had said that might be what was going on. She and I were getting to be good buddies, and I'd confided in her about all this.

Well, after reading about it, I just sat there in disbelief. It sounded exactly like what was going on. I had discovered this thing called sleep paralysis, or waking nightmares, where you're still partially in REM sleep when you're also partially awake. About 60 percent of people experience it at some time, and it's often accompanied by other things, like imagined speech and noises, intense fear, and even the imagined presence of a visible entity.

This was good news for me because it explained what had been going on, and it meant I wasn't really crazy, nor was there a Bigfoot haunting me. I was ecstatic and called my friend. We talked way into the night, and she gave me some good advice, saying maybe something was bothering me and manifesting itself like a big monster. She then added that the best thing I could do was face my fears, because then they would go away.

I went to bed really tired, but I also felt relaxed for the first time in ages, knowing that whatever was going on was something I could deal with.

That very same night, I had the nightmares again. But this time, they were even more vivid and real, and I awoke paralyzed with fear. A giant Bigfoot was trying to get into the house, and I was frozen and couldn't get up. I could hear it rattling the kitchen door, then I heard the sound of splintering wood, like it was breaking in.

I was finally able to move, and I slipped out of bed and opened the bedroom window and crawled out. I didn't have my car keys, so I ran to the neighboring house and was ready to start pounding on their door when I realized it all had to have been another dream. I should go back and see if there was anything broken before alarming everyone.

I stood there in the bushes, hidden, when I saw a shadowy figure walking down the alley. It was huge! I started shaking again. This was no dream, as there was no way I could possibly still be asleep or even half-asleep. I could even hear its footsteps as it walked away.

The thing was gone, and I finally crept back over to the house, where I could see my nightlight through the kitchen window. Everything looked OK, and the door was closed. I crawled back in through my bedroom window and quickly turned on the light, then went from room to room, turning on all the lights in the house.

When I finally worked up the courage to go into the kitchen, I saw that all was fine. There was no splintered wood, and the door was still locked. It had to have been a dream, even the shadowy figure.

I just sat there all night, trying to wake up and wondering what I should do to end this nightmare. I had to do something.

Then I remembered what my friend had said about facing my fears. What would be the scariest thing I could possibly do? I thought about this, then got my old sleeping bag and a pillow, some warm clothes, some food and water, and put them all in my car. I made some hot tea for my thermos and was soon on a back road, heading for the nearby mountains. I didn't want to waste any time fixing this problem. I was going to go face my deepest fears.

It was Saturday, so no one at school would miss me. I hadn't told a soul where I was going because I didn't know where myself. All I knew is that I had to face my fears, and for me, the scariest thing I could do would be to go camp all alone in Bigfoot territory.

I drove and drove until I was in about as remote an area as you can get without high clearance. I had worked my way up into the mountains until I could go no further on an old road, and I stopped in a little clearing in the timber.

It was beautiful up there, and it looked like no one had been there for years. I hadn't been out in the woods like that for so long, and I wondered how I could get so removed from nature, which I loved. I vowed to start camping and getting out more.

It was soon evening, and I took out the stuff for sandwiches I'd grabbed from the fridge, eating a cold dinner. I hadn't even brought matches or anything for a fire, so I just sat there on a log until it got dark.

As the shadows lengthened, I started feeling insecure and wanted to flee and go home. But I had to see this through, even if it killed me. I couldn't live in fear any longer.

Looking back, I can now see that I was still in a disoriented state from the previous night's events and wasn't really thinking clearly. I could easily have been killed by a bear or mountain lion, but I didn't care.

Actually, I did care, but I was in denial, thinking I could stay out there and face my fears and come back unharmed. It's amazing how we sometimes just ignore the danger and carry on, which is what I did that night.

It was soon pitch dark with no moon, and I just sat there. I have no idea what time it was when I decided I should do this right if I was going to do it at all. I found a big stick and started whacking it on a tree. I'd read that Bigfoot communicates this way, through woodknocking.

I did this for a few minutes, then sat back down on the log, feeling like I must really be crazy after all. It was bad enough to come up here totally alone with no weapons, but it was truly insane to try to intentionally attract a Bigfoot to you.

I sat there in the blackness and started crying. I was so scared, and I hadn't asked for any of this. I had just innocently stumbled onto a topic that I found interesting, and now here I was, alone in a dark forest with who knows what. I might be dead before morning.

As I sat there, I heard it—woodknocking in the distance. I sat up straight. Woodknocking! I had to be imagining it. I stood up, thinking the motion would get the blood flowing through my brain and wake me up. I had to be dreaming again!

My instincts were to run and get into my car and drive off as fast as possible, but I just kept thinking of what my friend had said about facing your fears. But what if my fears were legitimate fears, the kind where your instincts are telling you you're in danger?

Now the woodknocking had stopped. I made myself sit back down, even though I wanted to run. I now made a wa-whoop noise, the kind I'd heard on an internet recording that someone had made of a supposed Bigfoot up in Washington or Oregon.

I did this several times, then was shocked to hear the same noise, though far in the distance, like the woodknocking had been. I was now trembling, and I couldn't have run if I'd decided to. I was frozen in fear.

What was I doing? What if this thing were real and not just my imagination? I would go down in history as one of the stupidest people on the planet—kind of like walking into a lion's den in the zoo. Fear had a purpose—it told you when you were in danger.

Face your fears, I told myself over and over. Otherwise you're going to be victimized by them for the rest of your life. I decided I would rather die here than be afraid and have nightmares forever.

So, I just sat on that log. I could now hear something coming through the timber, and it sounded like it was mad. It was crashing through the trees and underbrush as if it didn't even need to negotiate its way through them, it could go wherever it wanted. And it was coming at an amazing speed.

Once again, my instincts said to run for the car and get out of there. But once again, I could just hear my friend saying it over and over, "face your fears."

My heart was racing and I now felt cold and clammy. But I just sat there as this thing came for me, crashing along. Once it got closer, I could hear it making a low growling sound that sounded like a mix between a grizzly and an insane lunatic, a growl that said it wasn't real happy about me being in its territory.

Suddenly, all was silent. The noise had stopped completely. I knew it was upon me and had stopped, probably to assess the situation and figure out the best way to kill me. I was afraid to look up, and I just sat there looking at my feet. It was too dark to see anything, anyway.

I then heard a coughing sound. I knew bears made this sound, and I wondered if a bear was there, ready to attack me. I looked up. I was no longer afraid. If it were my time to die, so be it. Better dead than scared all the time.

I now saw it standing there, though all I could really make out were two glowing red eyes in the dark, eyes that stood a good seven feet above me. I sat there, looking at it, and it stood there, looking back at me.

I stood up, well aware of how small and puny I was in comparison, then I started talking to it. I was later amazed at the presence of mind I had to do this, but I was just no longer afraid.

I don't even remember what I said. It was some rambling thing about how scared it was making me and how I needed to be able to live a normal life and would it please just leave me alone. I went on and on and on and it just stood there, those glowing red eyes not blinking once.

It then turned and silently left, with no more of the breaking through the trees thing. Just like that, it was gone. I felt very peaceful and put my sleeping bag there on the ground, crawled into it, looked at the amazing stars above me for a few minutes, then was fast asleep. I knew I had hallucinated the entire thing and was actually as safe there as anywhere, maybe even safer.

I spent the next day just hanging around enjoying the peace and quiet of the high timber. I didn't hear one sound to remind me of people except for a couple of jets that flew high overhead. It was one of the most peaceful days I've ever had in my whole life, a peace that went way beyond the beautiful quiet place where I was.

I left that evening, needing food and water, vowing to come back often. It now seemed like a place of refuge for me, a place where I could always go and be safe and happy. I had been so scared the previous night, but like my friend had said, now that I'd faced my deepest fears, I was now rid of them.

I drove slowly back to Pocatello, happy for the first time in ages. I was eager to tell my friend that she'd been right, and yet I didn't want to talk to anyone and risk losing that deep feeling of serenity.

That night, I ordered a pizza and enjoyed sitting on my porch eating it. I then made a cup of hot tea and sat there outside in the dark, not a bit afraid.

I knew the Bigfoot had been my own imagination, my way of crystallizing my fears about life and failure and everything. It was just my way of dealing with things—to make them into a terrifying black monster instead of trying to actually solve the problems one by one. But it was now over, and I could move forward.

Imagine my surprise when the next morning I stepped out into the back yard and found wood splinters around the outside of the kitchen door jamb where something had tried to rip off the door. And imagine my even further surprise when I found several huge deep tracks in my back yard—Bigfoot tracks. I hadn't been hallucinating at all!

Would I have gone into the mountains that night had I known the Bigfoot that visited me was real? No, I don't think I would have, in fact, I'm sure of it—I'm not that gutsy. I really had thought I was imagining it all.

And as I stood there examining the tracks, I then knew that my fears had been legit and not all in my head. That made me feel much better about my instincts. The dreams hadn't been dreams at all, and they weren't a sleep disorder.

Funny, but knowing that gave me a feeling of relief and self-confidence. And knowing I had the courage to face my fears, even though I now knew they were based on reality, not my imagination, gave me even more confidence.

I have no idea if the original "dreams" I'd had were my imagination or not, but somehow I don't think they were. How could it be that I would continue to have Bigfoot sightings even after moving to Pocatello? I don't know, but I do know that the experience taught me something that will stay with me my whole life: we have to face our fears in order to live well and be happy, and there are many mysteries on this planet of which we have no real idea.

And now, as a teacher, I try to teach the children in my care both of those lessons and thereby enrich their lives. Maybe it will save them from going through what I did— mistaking reality for fears, and fears for reality.

The Thing in the Trees

This story struck me as pretty spooky, and it highlights the fact that not all Bigfoot are friendly like in Harry and the Hendersons. It makes me pretty wary of being out in the backcountry alone, and the storyteller's comment about how we shouldn't go looking for them may have merit.

I've heard of Bigfoot in the state of Arizona, but mostly up on the Mogollon Rim—but why not in the San Francisco Peaks? It would be good habitat, and parts of that area are pretty remote.

In any case, I heard this story around a campfire along the White River in northwest Colorado, and I noticed afterwards that everyone kept looking up into the trees, including myself. — Rusty

I hate telling this story. It still gives me the creeps after all this time, but I need to share it and get some feedback. I've told it to others, but they always just say I'm a good storyteller. They might just as well replace the word storyteller with the word liar. I know they don't believe me, and I can't say I blame them any.

I was in my twenties, and I was in great shape because I worked construction. On the weekends, I liked to hike and bike, so on top of work, I kept pretty active. This gave me a confidence that maybe wasn't really all that good for me, because I felt like I was invincible. Being at the peak of your physical abilities can make you feel like you can do anything, even though you can't.

I met a girl who I was instantly crazy about. My housemate said it was a case of matching dysfunctionalities, but he's always been a cynic when it came to relationships, so I ignored his advice about her being bad news. Turns out he was right, but I always learn things the hard way.

So, it was a Friday night, and I'd asked this girl out for dinner. We'd been out a number of times together and had fun, but this time we ended up having the biggest most raging fight imaginable, and it's a wonder we didn't kill each other.

I can't even remember what it was about now, but at the time, it seemed shattering. I think it had something to do with our different philosophies on getting married and having kids or something along those lines.

OK, so here it was, late evening, and I was totally upset and bummed out. I went home and threw some things into the back of my car and headed out.

I needed to go out to some place quiet and just think and be alone until I could figure all this out. I ended up splitting up with her, so you can see how serious a decision this was to me, because I really did feel like I loved her.

I was living in Flagstaff, Arizona, and I drove out by Sunset Crater into the Coconino National Forest. I kind of hesitate to mention where this happened, because I don't want anyone going out there searching for this thing— they very well might not come back.

Anyway, it was really late when I got there, and I threw my sleeping bag on the ground and just went to sleep. The forest there is basically ponderosa pines with a natural grassy understory, kind of like a big park. It's a really pleasant place—or used to be, anyway.

I slept OK, considering how upset I was. Well, actually, I kind of drifted in and out of sleep, waking up but not really, kind of like you would when you're sleeping with one eye open, so to say.

I woke up the next morning with the sun high and realized I'd slept in late. My watch verified this—it was ten in the morning! I got up kind of in a daze. I never slept that late, especially when camping, as I was usually up with the sun.

I had a power drink I'd bought at the convenience store on my way out of town, which is where I'd stocked up for the weekend—if you can call junk food stocking up. I'd been in a hurry, just wanting to get away as fast as I could.

I found a big volcanic rock and sat on it, drinking my caffeine, trying to wake up. Everything was so quiet and peaceful. It was already beginning to feel like nothing else mattered. I always felt that way when I got out in the backcountry.

As I sat there in the morning cool, I began to wonder why I couldn't just live out there. Why did I have to be part of society? I had no desire to prosper and get ahead, as they call it, which to me really meant just getting into debt and closing all your options by having to work. I'd never wanted a big house and lots of stuff.

I was perfectly happy just being outdoors with just the stuff in my car and on my back. Come to think of it, this attitude had been the root of all my differences with my girlfriend, as she was more normal, wanting a house and all that.

As I sat there on that rock, a nice cool breeze came up, and everything just felt perfect. It was then that I decided I needed to change my life. I would go home, break up with my girlfriend, and work really hard until I could afford a pickup with a camper on it, then I'd come back out and camp all the time, working just enough to resupply myself when needed.

This thought gave me the most peaceful feeling I'd had in years. I then recognized how truly unhappy I'd become in my own little version of the rat race. I was ready to leave right then and go home to start implementing my plan, but I knew I should wait until the weekend was over and just enjoy where I was since I was already there.

I went back to my car and grabbed the turkey sandwich and soda I'd bought, then wandered off, lost in thought. I could see my new camper in my mind, and I was already outfitting it and trying to figure out everything I might need.

Should I get a little solar panel to run the lights and all that? I would need to stock up on water jugs and maybe some extra jerry cans for gas. And how about some fishing gear? That's the kind of thing I was thinking as I ambled along, no idea where I was going, just wandering.

No, I didn't get lost, but it's a miracle I didn't, as I was paying no attention at all to where I was. But the San Francisco Peaks provide pretty good directional landmarks, and I'd hiked around there lots before, so I wasn't worried.

I came into a nice little open area and found another rock to sit on in the sun. It was a beautiful sunny day, and with my stomach now full, I was getting sleepy, so I just lay down in the tall grass and drifted off, nary a care. I'd already pretty much forgotten about my girlfriend, so that tells you how deep my so-called "love" for her must've been.

I have no idea how long I slept, but when I woke, I had an eerie feeling that something was watching me. I lay there still as can be. It felt really creepy, even though the sun was still just as sunny and the day just as nice. But everything had changed. I now had this really uneasy feeling.

Had I been having a bad dream? I couldn't remember it if I had. I lay there, trying to gather my thoughts a bit and see what was going on. Was it real or imagined? The hairs standing up on my arms felt pretty real, not like some dream or hallucination. It was a really intense sensation, one I'd never felt before.

I slowly raised my head and looked around, then I got to my knees and stood up, very slowly. It was then that I saw something, though I wasn't sure what it was. Heck, I wasn't even sure it was real.

There was something up in a big ponderosa pine across the little clearing from me—or was it just a shadow? It looked real, but I couldn't tell for sure, as it blended in with the big branches, but it looked like someone standing there on a branch, kind of leaning into the tree like it was trying not to be seen, yet watching me. Someone not really big, but yet not small, kind of the size of a small man.

I froze, pretending not to have seen it, and turned my head a little away, though I could still see it from the corner of my eye. Was it real? I couldn't tell, but it sure felt creepy. Why would I feel that way about a shadow? It had to be real, I thought, or I wouldn't feel that way, but I then talked myself out of it, as the shadowy figure didn't move, even though I sat there for a long time.

As I sat there, I started thinking about what it would be like to live in Africa, where monkeys hung around in the trees above you. This shadow was giving me the same feeling I would imagine you'd have when sitting out and being watched by a monkey sneaking around, a really bad monkey. Why did I feel like a shadow was out to get me? I didn't know, it just felt weird.

I finally decided I needed to get back to my car, as the sun was getting lower. I wasn't real sure where I was, but I knew it would take me an hour or so to get back. I wished that I hadn't wandered so far.

I casually started walking back the way I'd come, turning a few times to look again at the tree to see if anything had changed. Nothing looked different. I decided the stress was getting to me, and I just needed to get back to my car and have a good dinner. Maybe I was a bit dehydrated or something.

As I walked back, I couldn't shake the feeling that I was being followed, yet when I'd turn around, there would be nothing there. Of course, the trees could have provided good cover, but surely I would catch a glimpse if someone were following me, and I didn't.

I can honestly say it was the first time in my life I've been scared out in the forest alone, and the irony was that it was broad daylight and I'd really not seen or heard anything for sure. I decided it was my imagination, but yet I couldn't shake that creepy feeling.

Sometimes I wonder if we humans still have some of our natural wild defenses, if maybe some small amount of our instinct still serves us, some part of our senses that sends out the alarm when we're in possible danger. I really think that's what was going on, as I was soon to find that this shadow was real enough and meant me grave harm.

I got back to my car, somewhat shaken—why I didn't leave then is a mystery to me. I think it was because I refused to believe the thing was real—it was too out of my frame of reference, and I'd never seen anything out there before—in fact, I actually hadn't really seen anything, so why panic?

We hear about women's intuition, but I'm a guy, and yet I had a full-on intuition alarm. Maybe guys have intuition but don't pay it much mind, whereas women do. I don't know, but in retrospect, I should've left immediately. My gut feeling was to flee. Instead, I set to gathering firewood to spend the night. What an idiot.

It was soon dusk, and the creepy feeling had pretty much faded away, leaving me wondering what it had all been about. I felt better after eating a can of cold pork and beans on a bun, though that should've made me feel worse. Funny how things taste better when you're outdoors.

I settled back against that same rock I'd been sitting on earlier, pondering my fate and deciding to get a pickup and camper and go wild. I was again relishing that thought, feeling pretty carefree.

I eventually relaxed and got my old guitar out of the car and started strumming a few tunes, now seeing myself leading a cowboy kind of life, all the stresses of civilization forgotten.

As the stars began to come out in all their splendor, I sat there and composed a song about the western skies. Maybe I could make enough cash as a song writer to live on, even though I'd never sold a song in my life. Heck, that was the first one I'd ever even written. I thought about this later, and I think it was my mind trying to find a comfort zone to forget the stress from the shadow—for some reason, I was suddenly feeling very creative.

After a while, I put my guitar down and leaned my head against the rock, closing my eyes, fantasizing about hearing some of my favorite singers on the radio—guys like Waylon Jennings and Kris Kristofferson—and I imagined I could hear someone singing the tune I'd just written. And now the radio announcer was saying that Western Skies was the number one hit for that year, and he was cueing up another song by the same songwriter (me), saying it was destined to be another big hit.

Some country-western woman singer came on, and at first the song was really nice, something about big ponderosa pines, but then her mellow voice became a horrible screeching, ending in a scream that would raise the dead.

I woke with a start. I'd drifted off and been dreaming. Boy, was I glad that screaming was a dream—it reminded me again of Africa. But then, it happened again—there was something in the trees across from me making the creepiest sound ever, a sort of screeching screaming sound all rolled into one.

I jumped up and ran for my car, diving inside and locking the doors. Now, why I didn't just drive off then is yet another mystery, but I think it was because I didn't want to leave my guitar, and I was too scared to go grab it and run. That old Gibson had belonged to my dad, and it was about all he'd left me. He'd died in an accident, and that guitar meant a lot to me.

So, I sat there in the car, scared to death, wishing I'd had the presence of mind to grab it and wondering if my life was worth losing for a dumb guitar. I knew it wasn't, but I just couldn't force myself to leave.

It was now almost dark, and I knew I needed to get that damn guitar and get the hell out of there before it got any darker. I wouldn't be able to see anything then and would be even more vulnerable. I still had no idea what I was dealing with, but I knew it was something that could scream bloody murder, and I was sure that's exactly what it meant to do to me.

I finally worked up the courage to unlock my car door and slowly pull on the handle. I would jump out, run and grab the guitar, then get back in and peel out and leave. I had to go now or never. I was in good shape and could run fast, and I knew I could pull it off, if I could use the element of surprise.

As I opened the car door, I looked up at a small tree about ten feet from my car, and there, silhouetted against the darkening sky, was something in the branches.

All I could make out was a black shape. It was standing on a big limb, swaying with the tree in the evening breeze. I knew it was waiting for me, and as soon as I got out of the car it would jump on me.

I slammed the door and locked it again, then sat there in shock, suddenly feeling cold all over. At this point, I still hadn't got a really good look at it. All I knew was that it could climb trees and wasn't really big, but had a huge and very vivid terrifying scream. I had no idea what I was dealing with, which made it even more mysterious and frightening.

Well, I hadn't been paying attention to the weather at all, and now it was turning bad. I normally would've got a weather report before heading out into the woods, but this had been a last-minute trip.

Apparently a big storm was brewing, because the evening breeze was beginning to turn into a regular wind. I was amazed at how fast it had picked up, and it wasn't long before it was blustering pretty good and getting stronger by the minute.

Why didn't I leave? I was obsessed with getting my guitar back. I guess I can be pretty stubborn, and this was feeling like a life-threatening event, but yet I still wanted that stupid guitar. Well, I guess it wasn't the guitar that was stupid, but me.

I slowly turned my head to where I could see the tree this thing was in, somehow thinking if I acted all nonchalant it wouldn't know how scared I was. Maybe it would be gone, I hoped, but no, I could still see the outline of its head against the sky.

I was tired and hungry and wanted to leave, and yet I felt frozen in place. I had to get my dad's old guitar. There was no way I was leaving it there.

By then, it was almost dark, and the wind was now howling, gusting and rocking the car. The tree the creature was in was starting to bend in the wind, and I wondered if the thing would be able to stay up there much longer.

I don't know where it came from, but a thought came to me—start up the car, turn on the lights, honk the horn like crazy, then run and get the guitar. Maybe the surprise factor along with the wind would keep the thing in the tree from doing anything.

In retrospect, it was about as stupid a plan as I'd ever come up with, if you could even call it a plan. I started up the car, unlocked the door, kind of held my breath, honked the horn, then jumped out, ran to the rock, grabbed my guitar, and ran back to the car, all in what felt like a split second.

I felt a thrill of exhilaration and adrenalin all mixed together. I'd done it! I was safe back in the car and had the guitar. I started backing out to get onto the main road, and as I did so, I felt something heavy land on the roof of my car. I then knew the thing had jumped from the tree.

Crap. Why didn't I park heading out? I had to do a three or four-point turn to get out, and while I was doing this, the thing was on the roof, scratching the metal with what must have been long sharp claws or nails, like it was trying to dig a hole through and get to me.

What had been an intense situation was now becoming unbearable. My heart was racing and I wondered if I might pass out. It was like when you drink one too many power drinks, too much caffeine and ginseng. I was as wired as you can get.

I finally managed to get turned around and onto the main road, which was really just a rough dirt two-track. Now I was heading out, though I couldn't go too fast because of the ruts. Just then, something came over the front of the car onto the hood. It was then that I finally saw what had been terrorizing me for hours.

OK, I'll tell you what it looked like. The hair was brown and long, maybe several inches, and silver-tipped, like a silver-back gorilla. It had a dome-shaped head, with black eyes like pools of tar, but with a very intelligent look to them, though it was a threatening look, like it wanted to harm me, like it was angry.

I don't know what it was, but it fits the descriptions of a Bigfoot, though it was much smaller. Maybe it was a young one, a teen, or maybe it was stunted from something like lack of food, or maybe it had some kind of disease. Why wouldn't Bigfoot get diseases like humans do? In any case, it was different, and yet similar to the accounts I've read.

Seeing that thing made me realize what a fool I'd been to think I was invincible, to run and get the guitar and risk my life. I should've just left it there in the first place. Odds are good I would never have seen this thing and been traumatized.

Anyway, the thing was now on my hood, right smack in front of me, blocking the view so I couldn't see where I was going, forcing me to slow down. And as I did so, it began pounding on the windshield, trying to break it and get in, seemingly oblivious to the fact that it was on the hood of a moving vehicle.

I had to do something before it broke in, and there was every indication that it could easily do so. I slammed on my brakes, and it rolled a little to one side, and that's when I jerked the steering wheel as hard as I could, making it roll off the hood completely, although it felt like the howling wind had helped push it off. I whipped the wheel back the other way, then peeled out, now that I could see where I was going.

My hands were so clammy and wet that I could barely hold onto the steering wheel, but I managed to straighten the car back out and head down the road as fast as I could without wrecking.

The thing was gone.

I drove on and on, continually looking nervously in the rear-view mirror, expecting it to follow me or still somehow be on the car. I didn't stop until I got back to Flagstaff, then I pulled over at a diner and went inside, wanting the security of people around me.

I ordered a hamburger, but I really just wanted to be indoors where I felt safe. When my order came, I felt my hands shaking so much that I could barely hold onto it. I don't even remember tasting it or anything, I felt like I was in shock.

I then sat there for a while, not wanting to go back outside into the darkness. I had a strong urge to yell at everyone and tell them that the world wasn't what they thought it was, but I managed to keep quiet. I felt like I was in a dream, and everything felt off kilter.

I felt that way for days, maybe even weeks, and I had nightmares for several years after that. I'd been terrified that night, but the real damage came from the shift in my worldview—I no longer felt safe, nor did I feel like Planet Earth was what I'd thought it was.

It was a strange and hostile place for me after that, and I always walked around looking over my shoulder. I was a basket case for many years, and my dream of getting a camper and pickup dissolved into nothingness and was replaced by a deep fear of the wilderness.

I finally took up some outdoor sports, but I refused to play golf, even though most of my friends did. Golf courses were too much like the wilds, too many places for strange things to hide. I know everyone thought I was nuts, but they hadn't seen what I had.

I did finally manage to get back to what some would consider a normal lifestyle, though I never was much for being outdoors after that.

So that's my story, and after this experience, I have only one word of advice—you should never go looking for them. Trust me on this one.

The Logger

I hear a lot of crazy stories, most of which I know can't possibly be true. One rule that I have for putting a story in my books is that it be a first-person experience, as I can then usually tell whether or not the storyteller is pulling my leg.

The following story was told over a campfire in the heart of some of the best flyfishing in the world—the Yellowstone River. Even though it's a second person story and maybe a bit far-fetched, I'm including it here because if it is true, it illustrates a side of Bigfoot that I find most interesting—a desire to have a home, just like that of most humans. —Rusty

My grandpa's name was Jace, and he was old-school, the kind of guy who was self-reliant and independent. He told this story so many times I have it memorized.

It seems pretty crazy, but I know it's true because when I was in my 30s he took me and my dad to the site of his old cabin, and we then went back into the forest, and he showed us where the logs had ended up. Some were still there, though rotten by then. No human could have possibly carried those logs off like that.

This happened in the 1940s. My grandpa was living near Yreka, California, working as a logger, staying on-site in an old canvas cabin tent way out in the sticks. My grandma and their three kids lived in town in a rented shack.

After a while, my grandpa managed to buy a cheap piece of land. He wanted to build a house, something nice, for my grandma and the kids.

This land was about as far out in the sticks as the logging camp, that's why my grandpa could afford to buy it. It was cheap. No electricity, and the only water was a little stream running through the corner of the property. I guess they call it being out in the sticks because you are, you're right in the middle of a bunch of trees—big sticks.

After he bought the land, Grandpa started accumulating stuff for what would be their log cabin. He would buy scrap logs from the guy he worked for, then haul them out there in his pickup. We're not talking huge logs here, but they were substantial enough to make the walls of a small house.

Well, after some time, he finally got what he needed to start the cabin. He built a foundation of rocks, then borrowed a truck with a hoist on it and started on the walls.

I don't know much about log construction, but what he said he did was basically notch the ends, then stack them on each other, using the notches to hold them together. It's pretty much an old-style way of construction, and I think a number of old notched cabins are still standing all over the country.

He would go out there on the weekends and work on the cabin, camping out. He didn't see much of Grandma, but it was OK because he was building them a house of their own. It was a pretty exciting time for them.

Keep in mind that back then, zoning and codes and ordinances and inspections didn't exist—you could just go out and build whatever you wanted.

Well, one night Grandpa had a visit from an unexpected guest. He woke up in the early morning hours, sometime around four a.m., to the sounds of something big scuffling around the site.

He at first thought it was a bear, which is pretty much what everyone thinks a Bigfoot is until they actually see or hear it. Bears are much more common, and we have photos and first-hand accounts of them by the gazillions— but Bigfoot, not so much.

So, Grandpa gets up and sits there on the edge of his camp cot, listening, hoping it goes away and doesn't get into his cooler. Of course it finds it, and when Grandpa hears it over by the cooler, he decides to get out his .243 Winchester rifle and scare it off.

Well, before he could get the gun and get out of the tent, he could hear it tearing through the forest. It made a thumping noise, and it sounded like a man, as its stride sounded two-legged, not four. It had somehow known he was coming after it.

Grandpa shone his flashlight over to where the cooler had been, and it was completely gone. He'd never heard of a bear stealing a cooler—they usually tried to get into it, but to just carry it off was unheard of.

The next day, Grandpa worked hard and got the first course of logs up, all around the circumference of the house, one or two logs high. He was pretty satisfied with the amount of work he'd managed to get done, especially since all he had left to eat was some cheese and crackers. My grandpa was a hearty eater, and I can tell you that he would've considered cheese and crackers about the same as fasting. He finally had to go home early because he was hungry.

Every time he'd go out to the cabin site, he'd haul a few logs in his pickup, until eventually he had a pretty good pile going.

Well, one weekend he went back out there—I think this was a few weeks after the cooler incident—and he got out of his truck and just stood there, puzzled. Something wasn't right, but he couldn't quite put his finger on it.

But after a while, he figured it out. Some of his logs were missing! His log pile was a bit smaller. He said he walked around and around that pile, trying to figure it out, thinking he was maybe remembering wrong. He hadn't really been counting the logs—he knew he needed quite a bunch for the house but had no idea exactly how many— but he started counting them after that.

He scratched his head a bit, then went back to working on the cabin. It was hard strenuous work, especially trying to stack logs all alone, even with a hoist, but he was making good progress.

Another weekend over, and he was back to work that Monday at the logging camp. Now, the land where he was building the cabin was about ten miles as the crow flies from the logging camp, and he never put two and two together because of that distance, or so he said. But the guys had come back to the logging camp and found some full oil drums rolled over a small bluff downhill from the camp.

Oil drums are pretty heavy when they're full of oil, and nobody could figure out how this had been done. Of course, people later compared notes and found out that a number of logging camps in northern California had experienced such activity, though it seemed like it was more common in the 1960s than in the 1940s, when Grandpa was there.

Well, Grandpa returned to the cabin site that weekend with a few more logs, only to find that a few more had been stolen. But this time, he had a plan—he had brought some posts and a metal gate, and he set the posts in concrete and soon had a gate across the road that he could lock. That would end the theft, he was sure.

You can guess what happened next—a locked gate and yet still more missing logs the following weekend.

Now Grandpa was really puzzled. It would take a truck to haul off those logs. They weren't something one could just pick up and walk away with—or were they? Could the culprit be that big bear? This thought crossed his mind, but he recognized it as being ridiculous.

Bears didn't have thumbs to grab things with, and what on earth would a bear need logs for? The whole forest was full of logs. It seemed like it would be the last thing that something living in the forest would steal.

OK, so now he began sleuthing a bit. He looked all around the log pile for tracks, and sure enough, he found some. He said he wished later he hadn't found them and had dropped the whole thing, forgetting about a few missing logs and focusing on building the cabin. Of course, the way things were going, he could've tried to ignore it all, but sooner or later, he would have had to acknowledge that there was something out there when all his logs were missing.

The tracks were deep and large and had huge fat toes on the end. They were like nothing he'd ever seen, and he knew what bear tracks looked like. He sat down for a while, trying to clear his head, but then he got mad. Whatever it was, it was stealing logs he'd worked hard to get, logs he needed to make a home for his family. He needed to put an end to all this.

He went and got his rifle from the rack in his pickup, then started following the tracks. They were easy to follow, as they went right through the soft tuft in the forest. Someone trying to hide their trail would be more likely to walk down the little creek, but maybe walking down a rocky creek wasn't so easy when carrying big logs.

Grandpa followed the tracks until he suddenly felt a strange sense of dread. He said it just came over him all of a sudden out of the blue for no apparent reason, a feeling that he was going to die a really ugly death if he kept going on. Grandpa was terribly afraid of grizzly bears, as he'd been in Alaska and heard about how cruel they are when they kill, but there were no grizzlies in northern California.

He wasn't sure why he felt so afraid, but he followed his intuition and turned and went back to camp, wondering if somehow he hadn't unknowingly been tracking a grizzly. It seemed like a long way to go, but maybe a rogue grizzly had wandered down from Canada and made it in into the California mountains. There were plenty of places to hide near Yreka in the 1940s.

This thought gave Grandpa the creeps and he didn't sleep too well that night. He had no idea why he was so scared —it just didn't make sense. The next day he worked on the cabin some more, then left and went home early.

Now, my grandma was a very practical type of woman, and she just figured Grandpa was being jumpy, but she decided to go out to the cabin with him the next weekend. Her sister Jean would watch the kids.

So, that next weekend, the two of them went out to the cabin site. Sure enough, more missing logs. Grandma was getting frustrated with this whole scenario, as she wanted to move into her new house. She was tired of the run-down rental they were in, and Grandpa seemed to be taking longer than expected with the construction—and no wonder. It was this missing log thing that was tripping him up, and she was going to get to the bottom of it.

Grandpa again got his rifle, and the pair began following the tracks. They followed them for a while, and then suddenly Grandpa again got a feeling of doom and dread. He stopped and refused to go any further, but Grandma kept going, against his wishes. She was a feisty gal.

Grandpa sat there on a tree stump, feeling doomed and also feeling like a failure for letting Grandma go on alone, and he finally got up and began to follow her. He stole quietly through the thick understory of shrubs, making his way alongside the big tracks.

When he finally came to a small clearing, he stopped dead in his tracks. There stood Grandma, a ways out in the small meadow, examining a structure that looked a lot like the log cabin he was building.

The logs were stacked on each other in a square pattern just like someone was trying to imitate his construction.

The only problem was, these logs hadn't yet been notched and were just laying on each other. It wouldn't take much to tumble them down.

This was where the missing logs had gone. But who had stolen them?

As he stood there watching, he could see movement in the trees kind of behind Grandma's line of sight. Something was coming. He raised his rifle to his shoulder.

His movement, slow as it was, alerted it to his presence, and it turned toward him as it emerged from the tree line into the meadow. What he saw was like nothing in his wildest imagination, and he involuntarily stepped back and nearly dropped his gun.

Grandpa described it as being a dark brown color, almost black, with its head set directly on its shoulders. It didn't have a bear-type snout, but rather a human-like nose, though it was flat. It looked like a huge football player wearing a shaggy coat and with oversized feet.

Just then, Grandma turned and saw it too, the snapping of branches making her aware of something coming. She gasped and fell to her knees in sheer terror.

"Get up, Maggie, and run!" Grandpa yelled. Grandma hadn't known he was there, and his voice gave her the courage to stand and then run towards him as a giant black creature came towards where she'd been moments before. It made no motion to follow her, but acted like it instead was going to the cabin it had built. They could now see it was carrying a log.

As it crossed the meadow, Grandpa noted it had a stride that was at least three or four feet long. Its feet were huge, and it was shaggy and had long arms—and it walked on two feet, not on four, like bears do. The log seemed like nothing to it, a log that Grandpa would need the hoist to lift even a few inches.

Grandma was now by Grandpa's side, and as they watched, the creature walked to its cabin and placed a big log on top of another, making the wall taller. The wall was pretty shaky and looked like it would fall down any minute.

Grandpa grabbed Grandma's hand and rushed her along the way they'd come and back to the cabin, looking over his shoulder the entire time, ready to shoot, though he knew the rifle would do nothing to a creature that large. But it didn't follow.

They grabbed a few things and left. It wasn't long until Grandpa had sold the land, with the cabin and logs just as they'd left them that day. He later got a call from the buyer who was wondering why he'd been told there were logs on the property when there were none. Grandpa said he didn't know and let it go at that, but he knew where they'd gone.

It was also the end of Grandpa's logging career, which was probably a good thing, given how dangerous it is. He and Grandma ended up moving to eastern Oregon, where my dad was later born and where they started, of all things, a tree farm.

I now run that tree farm, a profession I really enjoy, though it's a lot of hard work. I guess I somehow owe it all to the log-stealing Sasquatch of Yreka, California.

About the Author

Rusty Wilson grew up in the state of Washington, in the heart of Bigfoot country. He didn't know a thing about Bigfoot until he got lost at the age of six and was then found and subsequently adopted by a kindly Bigfoot family. He lived with them until he was 16, when they finally gave up on ever socializing him into Bigfoot ways (he hated garlic and pancakes, refused to sleep in a nest, wouldn't hunt wild pigs, and on top of it all, his feet were small).

His Bigfoot family then sent him off to Evergreen State College in nearby Olympia, thinking it would be liberal enough to take care of a kid with few redeeming qualities, plus they liked the thick foliage around the college and figured Rusty could live there, saving them money for housing.

At Evergreen, Rusty studied wildlife biology, eventually returning to the wilds, after first learning to read and write and regale everyone with his wild tales.

He eventually became a flyfishing guide, and during his many travels in the wilds, he collected stories from others who have had contact with Bigfoot, also known as Sasquatch. Because of his background, Rusty is considered to be the world's Bigfoot expert (at least so by himself, if not by anyone else). He's spent many a fun evening around campfires with his clients, telling stories. Some of those clients had some pretty good stories of their own.

This is the eighth book of Bigfoot stories that Rusty has collected from around the campfire, available as ebooks at yellowcatbooks.com and from your favorite online bookstore. They are also available in print at Amazon.com.

Suspend belief and go on a road trip with a Bigfoot in Rusty's book, "The Bigfoot Runes," an adventure like none you'll ever see again. One reviewer (unclesquirrel) says: "If you are a enthusiast of bigfoot this book is a great read! This author is a masterful story teller! I know I would love to sit around a campfire with him!"

You can follow and communicate with Rusty at his blog at rustybigfoot.blogspot.com. And check out Bigfoot Headquarters at yellowcatbooks.com.

Also, you'll enjoy "The Ghost Rock Cafe" by Chinle Miller, a Bigfoot mystery. Also available at the above websites.

Whether you're a Bigfoot believer or not, we hope you enjoyed these tall tales...or are they really true stories? Only Rusty and his fellow storytellers know for sure.

add logo

17741481R00170

Made in the USA
San Bernardino, CA
16 December 2014